14 Viney Hill

Also by this author

TravelWorks
HomeWorks
Oh, and another thing…

14 Viney Hill

Carole Susan Smith

Copyright © 2019 Carole Susan Smith

All rights reserved, including the right to reproduce this book, or portions thereof in any form. No part of this text may be reproduced, transmitted, downloaded, decompiled, reverse engineered, or stored, in any form or introduced into any information storage and retrieval system, in any form or by any means, whether electronic or mechanical without the express written permission of the author.

This is a work of fiction. Names and characters are the product of the author's imagination and any resemblance to actual persons, living or dead, is entirely coincidental.

The views expressed in this work are solely those of the author and do not necessarily reflect the views of the publisher, and the publisher hereby disclaims any responsibility for them.

ISBN: 978-0-244-18892-4

PublishNation
www.publishnation.co.uk

My first novel 14 Viney Hill is dedicated to my best friend, lover, partner-for-adventures and husband Terence Warrener Smith. Thank you, Terry, for everything.

About the Author

The opportunity to do many unusual things and to work in other countries, including Siberia, the Palestinian Occupied Territories, the Far East, across Europe as well as in the UK, provided the source for Carole's three light-hearted memoirs. This is her first novel which is entirely fictional ... probably.

Acknowledgements

I am indebted to Gwen and David Morrison at PublishNation for their expertise and support over the last six years.

14 Viney Hill

You may think that a rather ordinary suburban house like me would not have much to say, but I can assure you I've seen some things in the last hundred years or more that would amaze you!

The history of my part of town is quite fascinating actually. Viney Hill was built on what was formerly the vineyard for the Belvedere Estate. It would seem that a very fine Elizabethan Manor House was built here in 1588 by Sir William Cecil who was the Secretary of State to King Edward IV. Later, this gracious property was passed to Charles I for his French wife to live in. Queen Henrietta Maria lived in the Manor House until the outbreak of the Civil War in 1642 when she was moved away for her safety.

The property was, for a brief period, in the ownership of one General John Lambert who I understand was one of Cromwell's men. Then the house was bought by Thomas Osborne, the Duke of Leeds. He and his family lived there for many years. After the Duke's death in 1712, the house and land were totally neglected and everything slowly fell into disrepair. Finally, after two centuries, I'm happy to say that the whole area has been reinstated including the building of some new homes for wealthy people.

My small parcel of land is situated in the Parish of Wimbledon in the county of Surrey. At the turn of the century, this estate of luxury houses was built on what became Viney Hill, by a gentleman developer. Number 14 was one of them, although I was not completed until Christmas 1912. Each house is a little different, although you might not realise that from the exterior. The builders used London Brick which is available locally and these are a rich russet-red and appear to glow in the sunshine. I have a fine slate roof and a view from several of my windows across to the panorama of the city of London. As you might imagine, that view has changed a great deal over the years. At the time of my building, there were three reception rooms, intended to be useful for entertaining, and three bedrooms suitable for a growing family. There's a small garden at the rear and attached to the side of the house a lean-to with a water closet. The latter was the very latest design of the period, befitting an up and coming area like Wimbledon, given that these parts were becoming so much more accessible by tram and train.

My first occupants were Reginald and Maria Osborne (no relation to the Duke of Leeds, the surname was just a coincidence!). As a lawyer, Reginald's business kept him daily in London town, but he had decided it would be pleasant to live in this area especially as they were hoping to bring up a family in the countryside. Every day he would take the tram all the way to the Victoria Embankment for four pence each way. He was delighted to tell his colleagues how very pleasant and convenient this arrangement was, especially as his chambers were nearby the terminus at the Inns of Court at Temple.

Maria kept the home clean and tidy and when she had finished her chores she would sit in my garden under the sweet chestnut tree, reading or sewing.

During World War I, Reginald was exempted from serving in the armed forces because he was in a reserved profession. None-the-less, it was a troubling time for the Osbornes and both knew many young family members who went to fight for their country and never returned. In spite of this, before long, my rooms echoed to the joyful sounds of small children, laughing and playing. First a boy, Peter, was born and less than two years later a daughter, Emily.

The Osborne family lived here for over twenty years and were mostly very happy, apart from one deep sadness that cast a dark shadow over their time. Little Emily contracted poliomyelitis at the age of four, initially suffering paralysis and dying not long after. The couple were absolutely devastated and never really got over their loss.

Finally, in 1936, they moved away, leaving the house to their grown-up son Peter. He had followed his father into the legal profession and was determined to make good use of the property, considering that I was an asset, by letting out my rooms to other young men in the same line of business.

I am not really sure what went wrong but it would seem that Peter was rather too fond of drinking and gambling so this venture did not work out to be as much of a money-spinner as he had expected. By the beginning of World War II, I was offered for sale and he was happy to sell me as quickly as possible. He moved all his belongings - which were meagre as he had been selling items to fund his lifestyle - over to some rooms which were nearer to his chambers.

Bernard and Edith Elliott were delighted to move in. Bernard was the only son of Joseph Elliott, a tradesman who had opened a shop in the town. Over the years the business had grown into a thriving concern as a department store. Bernard had been running the business competently for many years since his father's death. This was a relatively gentle period in my life and the couple were kind and thoughtful. They had one child; a boy named David.

In contrast with my inside life, the exterior of number 14 lived through a truly shocking time. During World War II, the area was subjected to so many alarming aerial attacks. The newspapers called it "doodlebug alley" because of the number of bombs that the German pilots targeted on Wimbledon in an effort to disable Croydon airport nearby. I shall never forget the glow of the night sky on 6 November 1940 when a terrifying number of incendiary bombs were dropped. Many houses were turned to rubble including one very close by in Woodside Road. Wimbledon suffered death and destruction with more than 150 people being killed in the town during this dreadful war. I'm happy to say that I escaped without much material damage, although some of my roof slates were never the same.

Meanwhile, Elliott's Store went from strength to strength and became a landmark for local people and visitors alike. After Bernard's death in 1957, both number 14 and the business were handed on to the safe keeping of young David.

David was a hardworking and enterprising young man who was married to Annabelle. This was not a happy relationship and I often heard shouting and fiery arguments. It seemed that no matter what David did to please his wife, she was not satisfied. For example, she had complained endlessly about my old-fashioned outside toilet so this was dispensed with in favour of a more modern arrangement with one of my large bedrooms being converted to an indoor bathroom. Similarly, my small galley kitchen was not to the liking of the lady of the house but David put his foot down and refused to make further changes.

To be fair, he already had enough to deal with at the time and I overheard that there were money worries. This was exacerbated by a fire in the furniture warehouse in Gap Road which damaged or destroyed a substantial quantity of customer's goods. Eventually, Annabelle disappeared and I presume that she and David separated. He continued to live within my walls and although I had hoped he would find another partner, it never happened.

I saw very little of my next owner during the 1970s. James Henry Smith was a businessman and he had invested in number 14 for the sole purpose of making money. I was divided into four flats and each room was let to professional people working locally. In practice this was mainly young women teachers or nurses although occasionally a man would take up a room before embarking on a relationship with one of the other occupants. Mostly, they were well behaved and respected the house but that was in the early days.

I cannot say the same for Mr Smith's subsequent occupants during the next ten years or so. These were predominantly students and they were not nice people. Nothing too bad, you understand, but things like doors slamming which rattled my very innards and general neglect. For instance, no one ever seemed to do the washing up until the heap of dirty plates and mugs filled all the work surfaces. There was supposed to be a rota for taking out the rubbish but no-one seemed to care, even when there was an outbreak of rodents who came indoors to help themselves. It's a pity that the tom cat that used to live here was no longer around.

There were so many noisy parties where the young students' behaviour seemed to be out of control. Someone would hang some balloons out of my upstairs window, which was supposed to be a sign that anyone (even strangers!) was welcome to join the party. I was aware of much drug taking and drinking to excess. Mr Smith appeared to let this carry on, although I did witness one terrible night when the police were called to calm down a fight taking place in the street outside. It took me some time to understand what was happening but I gather that the table lamp showing prominently in the bedroom window and lit with a red bulb was in fact a sign that prostitutes were on offer. The man was a customer and he took issue with another man who was the young lady's pimp with the latter requesting payment for services rendered. The fight was not pleasant.

Finally, Mr Smith was taken to court himself for running a brothel although he managed to escape justice and subsequently sold me for much less than I was worth. At least, that was what he told the people who bought it.

After that tumultuous time, I began to feel some love coming back into the home. The new owner removed my old rotting wooden windows and replaced them with the very latest uPVC casements. Then he extended the old kitchen and installed a cooker, a washing machine, a fridge and freezer and some very smart cupboards. It was all quite an upheaval, with old flooring being removed and soft carpets laid in the remaining bedrooms. Part of this major refurbishment involved central heating and gradually I could feel warmth and kindness flooding back into the place.

Actually, I am not being funny but it turns out that my owner is called Trevor Love. It must have been a good omen because the atmosphere is so much more sympathetic. Mr Love has a sensible approach to selecting who he lets the house to and so he makes sure that everything is well kept and cared for. Most families have been keeping me in good condition and many remain for seven or eight years before moving on, I presume, to a house of their own.

After all those renovations there followed a succession of new occupants, all of whom benefitted from this work. Some of them even made some modifications themselves. For instance, the back garden, which had been neglected for far too long, was turned into an "entertainment" space with a patio and barbeque, a water feature and multi-coloured lights. I'm not sure it's to my taste, especially as they took down the old chestnut tree and dug up the rose bushes but at least it's loved and lived in.

Another couple renovated the old bathroom, getting rid of the avocado bathroom suite and installing a modern waterfall shower, WC and bidet in white, with bold red "accents".

The current family are definitely my favourites. The father spends a lot of time fiddling with the lighting and the electrics which deal with the doorbell. There are television screens in almost every room and I hear discussions about the quality of the broadband and internet access. There are no door keys, which is a blessing given the number that got lost by previous occupants.

The kitchen is what they call "state of the art" whatever that means, but I can tell everyone is happy here when they sit down to eat meals together. The mother is kind and cheerful. She clearly loves her husband very much, but I'm not going to divulge how I know! She goes out to work some days but at other times she sets the robot cleaner going and sings to herself as she tidies up after the children. They have two children, both boys, who are fundamentally well behaved although they can be boisterous, especially when they are playing with the dog.

This family has lived here at number 14 for quite a few years and I do hope they will stay.

2. Wimbledon

I'm pleased we chose this house because it is just the right size for the four of us and conveniently located for my three mornings a week office job and the primary school that the boys go to, as well as the station so that Tom can get into central London every day. In fact, we were delighted to find that we can walk from the house to everywhere that is important to us and that saves massively on travel costs. At the time when we moved here, the landlord - whose name is Mr Love - seemed a bit doubtful about us because it was obvious that I was going to give birth imminently. He didn't realise it would be twins, and neither did we.

The rent on 14 Viney Hill is quite high but manageable now we are both working. We have a friendly if informal agreement that we can decorate as we like indoors, as long as we keep it in good condition, generally cared for and not painted in exotic colours! Mr Love deals with maintenance of the exterior including the roof and the paintwork. I think we are supposed to do the garden but Mr Love cuts the small patch of grass anyway so there's not much effort involved for us. After several years living here, we feel it is our home even though we don't actually own a brick of it. Speaking of bricks, it was built in the early twentieth century of rich, red bricks which promise to last for many generations to come. The Hill is lined on both sides of the road with similar houses, many of which are multiple occupancy, except for the really palatial ones which we refer to as "millionaire's row". We are lucky to have the house to ourselves, even though it's not very big but it is just fine for us and it's also in a respectable area of the town.

I am pondering our good fortune because I cannot sleep. Something woke me up around four o'clock this morning and instead of going back to sleep immediately, which would have been sensible, I've been lying here allowing my over-active mind to think about various random unconnected things.

It's very quiet and peaceful here. I can hear the birds just starting up a modest dawn chorus, which I think is amazing for a city even if we are in the outer suburbs. I can picture the view from the bedroom window as if my eyes were fully open and I was standing in front of it. I can see miles across leafy South London, with higgledy-piggledy slate rooftops in the foreground and looking further on to the unmistakeable outline of the former Battersea power station and the city centre beyond. I have always appreciated London for its colour, variety and activity; I wouldn't want to live anywhere else now.

This restful thinking comes to a grinding halt as I remember that the smart business suit that I had intended to wear to an important client meeting later this morning is actually still at the dry cleaners. Damn! Now I will have to think of something else that looks business-like which isn't in the laundry basket. I used to be so organised and efficient before the boys were born but those days are long past.

As a recruitment consultant, I meet with clients to assess what skills and talents are needed by their business and then try to find suitable personnel by asking around my contacts, advertising vacancies and proactively headhunting. Today's client has emailed me an outline of the staff they will need for a new division of their company and is meeting with me to discuss the details. Any organisation wanting to expand is gold-dust to companies like mine, as genuine growth is rare following the Brexit shambles. You would think, a decade on, things would have got a bit easier but they haven't. So, I'll need to be on my best behaviour!

Tom doesn't say much about his work and he's much better than me at closing the office door and leaving it behind until the next day. He is an artificial intelligence developer and works for an IT company that specialises in home robotics. That sounds rather grand but his major contribution to date has been to enhance ALLEGRA, which he calls the great granddaughter of ALEXA. He's always bringing bits of technology home for us to try, generally before they work properly in my opinion.

I can hear some soft whispering which suggests that the boys are awake. Although identical twins, Logan and Theo are totally different. Logan is quiet and thoughtful – it will be him saying 'shhh…' – and Theo is excitable and often impatient. I love them both so much.

As the chatter gets louder, Tom rolls out of bed and with a finger to his lips and an exaggerated tip-toe into their room he asks the boys to keep the noise down. Tom is my best friend, my lover and an all-round super-star. I cannot abide those women who delight in criticising their partners to other women, nor those men who insist on using the phrase 'that will get me some brownie points'. Grow up people, treat each other as adults and value what you have, I think!

Eventually I conclude it is time to make a start to the day, although I am really tired now that I've wasted three hours' potential sleeping time by day dreaming. It is evident I am half asleep as I trip going in to the shower and stub my big toe. The pain is out of proportion to the size of the digit and I hop around trying to stem the blood. Tom asks if he can help and I snap back at him, which was really uncalled for. I give him a hug when I get out of the shower to say sorry for my short temper but he doesn't seem to appreciate the soggy cuddle.

Downstairs, I get breakfast ready for all of us. It's just cereal and a piece of fruit today. Theo bursts into the room shouting, 'make him give it back!' It turns out Logan is wearing Theo's school pullover and as I pointed out, as patiently as possible, their navy school uniform pullovers are exactly the same so it really doesn't matter. Logan is quietly digging his heels in and I just wish the day could have begun a little more serenely.

Just as some order is being restored, Tom manages to drop one of last night's dinner plates that he was putting back in the cupboard. It smashes to smithereens on the tiled floor with pieces flying all over the place including into Dog's food bowl. In case you are wondering, the boys absolutely insisted on naming the dog Dog. We argued cogently for something a little less prosaic but once the pair of them make up their minds there's little one can do. They giggled and giggled but were unmoved by our arguments. So, Dog it is. He's a wire-haired fox terrier with a face that will melt your heart and a friendly nature that works well in this family.

By the time I had moved Dog into the hall, swept up the broken shards so that no one got injured and thrown away and replaced the contents of Dog's bowl, it felt like it was going to be one of those days where you wish you could start all over again. If only. I suppose I should have realised that it was Friday the 13th, not that I'm superstitious in any way.

Tom apologises for the plate mishap and proceeds to finish his breakfast calmly, clean his teeth and pick up his iPad ready for the short walk and tube journey into the office. I could see we were going to be in a rush, so I give him a quick peck on the cheek and suggest he heads off before us. I hate being in a rush like this but at least we can have some quality time together at the weekend. Tom gives me a proper hug and as I smell his aftershave, I wish we didn't have to go to work today.

'Boys, get your bags and wait by the door please.' I rush upstairs grabbing a navy jacket and my briefcase, giving a quick glance to my appearance in the mirror as I slicked my favourite dusky rose lipstick in the general direction of my lips. 'Not bad,' I thought, smiling to myself with the thought that even though my mother (who is actually my grandmother, but that's another story) always used to call me Plain Jane, I usually manage to look quite presentable. I have no idea why she called me that. She implied, to anyone who had the temerity to ask, that it was a nickname. I don't think it was out-and-out cruelty, although any young woman with less self-esteem than me could have been psychologically damaged for life. She pretended it was a joke, but honestly just Jane would have done nicely.

Just as we are about head off for school, Theo reminds me that they will need dinner money for the month ahead. Of course, it is not actual money as both boys have cards for contactless payment. I don't let them keep them otherwise goodness knows what they would be used to pay for! Fortunately, their cards were found without too much problem.

We dash out of the door and head briskly along the road to Garfield Primary. At the gate, the boys scamper off to see their friends and I nod briefly to one of the other mums I know. She makes a beeline towards me while I am thinking I just don't have time for small talk today. 'Jane, I keep meaning to ask where you get your hair done, it always looks so nice.' My hair is mousey at best with an attempt at blonde highlights when both my hairdresser and I are in the mood, so I conclude this embryonic conversation is a precursor to something else. 'Oh, thanks Beverley. Do you want me to message you or shall I give you my hairdresser's contact details next week when I'm not in such a rush?' I say. 'Don't worry for now Jane, as I need to tell you about the vintage jumble sale we are organising too. I'll see you soon then,' says Beverley to my rapidly disappearing back.

Turning right out of the school gate and glancing at my watch at the same time, I realise that a) I had ten minutes to walk to the office, which was just about do-able and b) I had left at home a printout of the important papers that the client had sent for me to study in advance. Spinning round on my heels I make the instant decision to go back for them. It would be better to be a few minutes late than to risk a meeting without the salient facts in front of us.

It didn't take long to get back to the house as fortunately it is mostly downhill. Without the boys to slow me down I was in the door, patted Dog, snatched up the missing file and back on my way within no time at all. By the time I got to Wimbledon High Street I was somewhat out of breath but only a few minutes late. My office, set within the beautiful Wimbledon Library building, would be an oasis of calm and professional expertise, I thought. I will be able to convey just the right atmosphere of efficiency and interest to get things right. So there really was no need to hurry but all the same I found myself breaking into a run over the uneven pavement.

3. White

I have been lying very still for some time because I cannot work out what has happened to me or where I am. The first thing I became aware of was a thudding headache. That seems to have dissipated somewhat. To start with I was afraid to move my head as I felt so sick. I don't think this is a migraine as I've never suffered with that sort of thing in the past. So, what has happened to me? What can I feel apart from the headache? Beneath my body the bed is soft and smooth. This is probably nothing to worry about then.

I can smell something strange, however. It is neither lemon nor flowery but it's not unpleasant. I suppose it smells clean, like after I have just dusted the furniture. I think I can taste it too.

It is quiet here but there are some soft and unfamiliar sounds. There's a small buzzing noise which is low pitched and constant. I can also discern a slight hissing sound. I think that could be people whispering.

I am breathing as deeply and as smoothly as I can because it is all rather frightening and I am trying to steady my nerves. 'Get a grip, Jane,' I said to myself. 'Let's try and figure out what is happening. It might be a smart move to open your eyes you know.'

Slowly and with great effort I do just that. Everything I can see is WHITE. Totally and unremittingly white. I close my eyes quickly while I try to make sense of it. Right. Am I dead? Let's try again. Open eyes. Above me are white ceiling tiles. That's good. I'm probably not in the afterlife as I doubt they would have ceiling tiles. Open eyes again. Look to the left. It's a white painted wall. Maybe I'm in prison but I don't remember doing anything especially wrong recently. I still feel really dizzy when I move my head and as this is all very tiring, I think I will go back to sleep for a while.

I have been reviewing my situation while I have been dozing and it would be most logical to assume that I am in a hospital. I don't know why I didn't think of that before.

I open my eyes again and although virtually everything is white it does begin to look like a hospital room. Before I can do a more thorough check, a voice penetrates my emerging consciousness: 'Jane! Darling! We've been so worried about you. Yes. Yes. Fetch a nurse.'

I cannot see who is speaking but offer a weak smile as the person seems pleased and relieved that I have opened my eyes. Suddenly there are three people peering at me from above. I don't know any of them.

The nurse is wearing a white dress, white apron and a funny little white cap. She looks into my eyes and smiles. 'Very good, Jane. You have had an accident and you've been asleep for a while. Now you are awake we can work towards a full recovery.'

I do not feel like speaking so I close my eyes again to signal that I need to rest. The nurse speaks softly to the other people. 'Your daughter will probably sleep for quite a while yet. I think it is time you went home and got some rest yourselves. If there is any change, we will let you know. Perhaps you can come in at visiting time tomorrow afternoon?'

I listen to this with some amusement. She referred to me as 'your daughter' but those people are not my parents.

What seems like some hours later, I replay this episode in my head and I'm none the wiser. I open my eyes again and look around without moving much. There's a swishing sound and a different nurse enters the room. This one has a distinctive Irish accent. 'Hello Jane. How are you doing? Is there anything you need?'

I realise that I have not heard my own voice for some time as I croak the words, 'what happened to me?'

The nurse is kind but presumably not well informed because she explains that I was knocked down by a bus and I have been in a coma for several days. She offers me some water but I don't feel up to drinking it yet. Worse still, I do not know what she is talking about because we don't have buses anymore. In fact, buses and diesel vehicles were banned several years ago in order to reduce carbon emissions. Most people have electric cars and apart from the trains which run on hydrogen, public transport is mainly by eVTOL helicopters for those who can afford it.

I am offered a drink of water again after she has taken my temperature. 'Perhaps we can get you to eat and drink a little something a bit later,' she says as she leaves the room.

I don't like feeling so confused but I do at least realise that I am in the best place until I can look after myself.

I suppose I may have slept through the night because the next time I open my eyes the daylight is quite sharp, almost blue. I feel rather shaky but I slowly raise myself to sitting up in bed. Looking around I can see that I am in a small room with two doors, a high window and a wooden cabinet beside the bed. A machine with cables hanging loose beside the bed may well have been some kind of monitor which is no longer attached to me. Apart from that and the cabinet, everything is white. So, my powers of observation are reasonably accurate then.

The first nurse enters the room, looks at me and smiles. 'I think it is time you tried some breakfast, young lady.' Before I have time to respond she departs, obviously busy and needing to attend to other patients.

I can hear a trolley being wheeled down what I am guessing is the corridor outside. The person pushing it lacks any refined steering skills and crashes it through the door into the room. I don't get a chance to speak before she places in front of me a bowl of soggy cereal, a banana, a mug of tea and what purports to be a slice of toast which probably had a fleeting acquaintance with a toaster some hours ago. 'There you are,' she says as she crashes back out of the door.

Actually, although it looks ghastly, I do manage to eat most of it and drink the tea. Most mornings my beverage of choice is coffee but under these circumstances I am happy to put up with this. I place the used plates and cutlery carefully on the bedside cabinet and wonder where my phone is. I really should phone home and make sure the family knows I am alright.

4. My New Life

The next time a nurse comes into my room I ask if I could have my phone. Her answer puzzles me. It seems that there is a "pay phone" in the main corridor but I would need to make sure I had the correct coins to use it. She did not seem to understand when I asked for my iPhone. She said that my belongings might be in the bedside cabinet although she thought the emergency services had to cut my clothes off me when I was brought in after the accident so there might not be anything wearable.

After she left the room, I searched inside the cupboard but all I could find was a strange pink and blue leather purse, with some foreign coins in it. The paper note with brown swirly patterns on it ("I promise to pay the bearer ten shillings"?) looked vaguely familiar but I put the purse back as it was not mine. There were no clothes either but at the moment this was the least of my worries.

Just as I was trying to make sense of this, there was knock at the door and without waiting for a response two women came in, preceded by another trolley. I noticed, almost subconsciously, that they were much better at manoeuvring this vehicle than their colleague with the breakfast trolley. They announced that they were the WRVS shop. I asked what WRVS was and rather amused they explained they were the Women's Royal Voluntary Service, which left me none the wiser. 'Do you want anything from the shop today, dear?' one of them asked. I glanced at the assorted boxes of tissues, bars of purple foil-wrapped Cadbury's milk chocolate and a selection of birthday cards, magazines and newspapers.

How very odd it all was. Does anybody read newspapers these days? I always go on-line for my daily dose of headlines. In fact, I have not looked at a magazine for years either, as all my favourite reading is on my Kindle. Tom teases me for using such old-fashioned technology but I don't care.

I take a second look at a newspaper, which seems to be reporting unexpectedly heavy snow in the north of the country. My eyes fall on the date.

MONDAY 23rd MARCH 1970

I feel sick. Silently, I shake my head at the WRVS women and they leave with a cheery smile and 'see you tomorrow, then'.

To begin with I just don't know what to think. I am stunned to my very core. If it really is 1970 (good grief, that's back in the twentieth century!) then it would explain why so many things seem wrong. It doesn't explain why I am here nor who I am. People have been addressing me by name and they seem to know me, even the couple who claim to be my parents.

Before I have time to think this through properly, I have a new visitor. She is about my age, although I'm not even sure what that is now, is well built, quite tall with blonde hair and a gentle smile. She does not seem perturbed that I have to ask her name and she explains she is Kate, one of my flatmates. The hospital staff have told her that I have short-term amnesia following my accident and may be a bit confused. Kate helpfully describes my other flat mates who are, apparently, Sue with short, dark curly hair and Angie with mousey hair. She explains that we live not far away from the hospital, in Viney Hill, in Wimbledon. On the one hand I am pleased but on the other I feel even more confused. When she pauses for breath, I decide I may as well find out the worst. 'How is Tom, please?' I ask.

'Oh, he's certainly missing you,' said Kate. I am beginning to feel relieved until she adds, 'I can't say we are happy about the little gifts he keeps bringing in though!' I don't know what she is getting at and so I venture, 'Could he come to see me, do you think?' Kate laughs.

'I think we are stuck with the rodents for now. I don't imagine they would allow cats in the hospital, even at visiting time!'

She pats the bed clothes and suggests that I should probably rest now. She hands over a shopping bag. 'Here's some of your clothes Jane, for when you are ready to come home. I'm happy to collect you, if that's helpful.' She leaves before I have time to ask anything else.

I sink back into the bed and feel like crying. Everything is wrong and I don't know what to do.

I blink away my tears as a nurse bustles in. 'How are we today?' I'm not sure I could give any kind of polite or coherent answer but it is obvious she is not expecting one. 'If you feel up to it you could use the bathroom, have a wash and comb your hair.' She points at the other white door which I had almost forgotten. I nod in agreement. Perhaps I will feel better if I freshen up.

Very gingerly I swing my feet to the ground and pause to make sure my legs, which are feeling quite wobbly, will hold my weight. So far, so good. I cling onto the bed and the cupboard as I make my way round the small room and open the door into the even smaller bathroom.

I use the WC and start to feel that I am in control again. I stand up and peer into the mirror over the hand basin. The person who looks back is me, but not me. Focussing on my hair causes a sharp intake of breath. What!! Where did those curls come from?! On closer inspection I can see that it is my face, my hair etc but the latter has been subjected to a very tight curly perm which is almost African in its intensity. On my right temple is a vicious looking scar about five centimetres long, which has been stitched with black thread and is surrounded by a colourful bruise. I look very carefully again and decide that the face looking out is definitely me, apart from the hair style. I wash my hands, splash my face with water and pat it dry with the paper towels that are sitting on the shelf nearby. I make my way back to the bed and close my eyes.

The next time I open them I find I am being watched, silently, by the couple who think they are my parents. They both look relieved when I open my eyes. For an instant I wonder whether to challenge their assertion that I am their daughter but as soon as the idea enters my mind, I realise that it would be cruel and would achieve little.

'Hello,' I say sleepily.

'How are you feeling today, Jane?' asks my imposter father in such a kindly manner. I don't think I could disappoint him by voicing the confused and angry words in my head.

'Well, I am feeling a bit better physically thank you. Unfortunately, I have a complete blank in my mind about who I am, what I do and where I live. It's really rather upsetting.'

Imposter mother immediately jumps in to make a comment. I have only known them since yesterday but I notice she rarely lets the man speak.

'Of course, dear. They said you would have short term memory loss. I should think amnesia is quite normal under these circumstances.'

I take a deep breath and decide I can make use of these imposter parents, to corroborate the things that Kate told me. 'So, can you tell me where I live and what I do?'

'You have a very nice flat in Wimbledon that you share with your friends. We don't go there very often as you are all so busy with your own lives.'

I detect an element of resentment there and I don't want to get involved with family politics, especially as they are not my family.

'Tell me about the flat and my friends please. I'm sorry to ask but it is a total blank to me.'

Imposter mum begins to reel off a lot of not very useful information about the places I lived before moving into this flat but after I have redirected her attention to the here and now, (my goodness, what a funny phrase that is under the circumstances!) she confirms some of the facts for me. These are heavily influenced by my imposter mother's personal opinions. For example, Kate is 'quite nice but a bit flighty' (whatever that means) 'and her room is on the ground floor like yours. Of course, we have never been in it.'

'Your flat is the best,' so says imposter mum who might just have a biased viewpoint. 'It's very comfortable. Of course, we gave you most of the furniture so apart from that ghastly sofa that you insisted on buying it is all quite tasteful.'

'The kitchen is nice but a little small if the four of you are in it together although the meals rota seems to help with that.'

'Upstairs is where Angie and Sue live. I'm not sure about Sue as she is so quiet and says very little.' Forgive me, but at this stage in the conversation I have a suspicion that Sue would have little opportunity to contribute once my imposter mother is in full flow. 'Angie is lovely and she always makes us a nice cup of tea on the rare occasions we are invited.' Ouch. This could prove difficult if I'm stuck with these people. 'Then you have that enormous bathroom which I'm sure is alright except in the winter months.'

Deep breath again. Let me try to sort something out. I know that Tom is a cat and not the dearly loved husband that I am missing so badly. 'What about the children?' I hear myself say, afraid really to know the answer in case they have transmogrified into pets too.

Imposter Dad at last gets a word in edgeways. 'Now then Jane, you must not worry about them. We know you are very conscientious but they will be fine until you are ready to go back.' That does not really clarify anything and I'm beginning to get impatient. I want to go back. I want to go back now. I want to go home to my husband and children. Suddenly I can feel a tear rolling down my face as I think of them.

Imposter Mum cannot resist using this to serve her own purpose. 'Now look what you have done. You've upset her. It's hard enough for her without you causing trouble.'

'No, I am alright really. I did want to know about the children though. I have been worried about them.'

'You will be back at school as soon as you are fit and well. Fortunately, your accident happened before Easter so you have all the holidays to recover.' I feel shocked and terrified by this last piece of information. Am I a pupil? Am I supposed to be a teacher? I'm both puzzled and appalled. Imposter Mum rambles on but at least she clarifies one thing. 'I think your classes have sent you a get-well card. It was posted to the flat.'

Changing the subject but with barely a breath to indicate a new direction, imposter mother asks: 'Now, when you are better, would you like to come home with us?' I cannot think of anything worse but I do not want to be seen as rude. 'Thank you,' I manage a small smile, 'but Kate has already brought in some of my clothes and has offered to collect me when I'm ready to leave. I shall be fine in the flat.'

I am now at the point when I need to process all this new information and luckily there is a ringing sound which I assume signals the end of visiting time. Saved by the bell!

'Thank you both for coming to see me. If there is anything you think might help trigger my memory, I would really appreciate that.'

I hope I have not got myself into more trouble by that request but I really cannot imagine how I can cope on a day-to-day basis while I find out how to get home to my own time unless I know more about my new life and who I'm supposed to be.

5. Wimbledon Too

A doctor called in to see me during his ward round and has decided that I can go home later today. My injuries have turned out to be relatively superficial, just bruising all over my body and the head injury. In his opinion, my mental recovery will be improved by being in my own home. That would be logical if indeed it is my home but I am not taking anything at all for granted right now.

I am also dreadfully worried about the cost of this private hospital room. I am not sure my health insurance will cover it. Tom and I chose the cheapest tariff as it's so costly now that the state-run NHS has been dismantled. They said at the time that it was because of Brexit but I never believed that. Anyway, we will just have to find the money somehow. I then stop myself pursuing this train of thought because I remember that I appear to be in some past time where this may not be a cause for concern.

So now I have spent half the morning in bed and the other half sitting in a chair which they have helpfully brought in for me. The nurse suggested I should get dressed ready for when my flatmate comes to collect me this afternoon, so I open the bag Kate brought in. I find some underwear which does not look familiar, a pair of bottle green tights, a pullover and a long tweed skirt along with some hideous platform shoes.

This presents me with a set of dilemmas. How do I feel about wearing underwear that might belong to someone else? I take the bra and panties cautiously to my nostrils and sniff. Well, they smell clean so I guess I may as well wear them. I try on the pullover and skirt which both fit me perfectly. Just as I am getting accustomed to this, the WRVS ladies arrive. 'Ooh very trendy that maxi skirt, dear. Did you want anything from the shop today?' I declined the offer and set about squeezing my feet into the multi-coloured platform shoes. In fact, they fit just fine but I have reservations about trying to walk in them. Apart from the fact that I hate them, I fear I shall break an ankle as they feel vertiginous. Still, I have no alternative footwear so I practice walking around my small room.

I am under the impression that the hospital needs to re-use this room shortly because a nurse asks me if I would like to move to a waiting room, which I have no objection to. At least it's a different view out of the window. There's not much to do here so I read a couple of Woman's Weekly magazines that were lying around and a copy of The Sun newspaper. I discover that the popstar David Bowie has just got married and that Ireland won the Eurovision song contest with a song called "All Kinds of Everything". The latter was held in Amsterdam and the young singer was called Dana. The magazines offered little more information as I was not especially interested in recipes or knitting patterns.

Looking out of the window I see the sky is blue, with small fluffy clouds. Is this the same sky that Tom and the boys are looking at?

A young man joins me in the waiting room for a short while. He has come to collect his mother who is recovering from a minor operation. He recounts the news that Concorde has achieved a supersonic flight. As I am not really sure what Concorde is, it's a strange conversation. I realise how ill-equipped I am for life in 1970.

Eventually, Kate appears at the door all smiles. 'Right then Jane. It seems we've been given the green light. Let's go!' I am warming to Kate by the minute.

It takes us some time to walk down the echoing corridors before we reach the hospital exit. Out in the fresh air, I breathe a sigh of relief that I can at last have a little more control over my destiny. As we approach the car park, I give a chuckle. 'Wow. It looks like a vintage car rally!' I say, before I could censor my mouth. Of course, all the cars look really ancient to my eyes but Kate would not realise why.

She looks at me strangely so I point to something that is possibly older than many of the other cars, in order to cover up my gaffe.

This is going to be really difficult. One option is to explain that I am not actually from this time but from the future. As soon as I consider it, I realise it would sound so bizarre that Kate might immediately walk me straight back into the ward. For the time being I will have to keep up the pretence of amnesia.

On getting into Kate's car I was disconcerted to discover that there are no seat belts. Kate asks what I am looking for, so I explain. 'Oh, it's not compulsory for older cars like this. I expect they will change the law at some stage.'

The drive to the flat is a source of great interest. To start with, I am amazed by the traffic density and the number of different kinds of vehicles on the road. Amongst them are cars, vans and lorries as well as black taxi cabs and red London buses. The traffic noise is deafening compared with the virtually silent electric vehicles I am accustomed to. The smell of partly burnt fuel and exhaust fumes almost makes me choke. I guess that all these vehicles are using the internal combustion engine. I cannot see many people walking and as far as I can tell, all the drivers are actually steering the cars themselves!

Kate seems like a good driver but even changing gear manually requires from her a level of concentration I am not used to, so I tried not to distract her by talking. It made me giggle (silently) when Kate was about to turn left, because there's a little knob in the middle of the dashboard which she turned and out pops an orange flipper at the side of the car. It did strike me as amusing anyway.

Pedestrian crossings seem to be different too and at least one that we pass is marked by a bright orange globe on top of a black and white striped pole. I wonder to myself how they are supposed to be used. The shops we pass look quaint and quite dowdy to my eyes. Young women in the streets, and possibly young men, are wearing long flowing gowns and virtually all of them have long hair. Other young women are wearing very short skirts in bold colours and thigh hugging boots. If I had been visiting another country, I would probably explain my reactions as "culture shock".

The other thing I observe is that people's heads are raised and they are smiling and looking at each other. It is a potent reminder that they don't have mobile phones in this time, not something I will forget in any case.

Eventually we drive along Wimbledon Parkside and seeing the familiar trees and paths across the Common I begin to feel reassured that I can at least recognise where we are.

Finally, we turn into Viney Hill and I sit forward in my seat to see where I live. We park outside number 14 and I am ridiculously happy to see that it is the house I know. The front garden is unkempt, the hedge needs cutting and the doors and windows have peeling pale blue paint but otherwise it is my home. At least, I'm guessing that it is what my home was like in 1970 not the home I lived in before all this happened.

Kate beeps her car horn and two people emerge almost immediately. I could see they were Sue and Angie from her descriptions. 'Welcome home!' said Angie. 'Yes,' said Sue, 'I hope you will soon feel better Jane.'

'Thank you. I'm sorry I don't remember anything. I don't honestly recognise you all either, but I hope my memory will come back soon.' I feel quite a fraud but I have no idea how else to deal with the situation.

'Don't worry,' said Kate, 'let's show you round and we can sort of pretend you are our new flatmate' as we walk through the door into the hall.

Immediately I recognise the black and white floor tiles although the furniture is old fashioned dark wood and not at all what I expect to see. On the left-hand side of the front door, fixed to the wall, is a large grey metal telephone box with a central dial and an enormous, to my eyes, handset like the sort you see in old films. Kate points to a door just beyond it. 'That's my room.'

Ahead is the kitchen. It really is quite small, just as my imposter mother suggested, so it was too cramped to fit us all in. There is a two-ring gas cooker and a Belfast sink but there does not seem to be a dishwasher, a washing machine or any electrical appliances at all. There is a large cupboard with an enamel drop-down work surface with cupboards above and below and little glass windows in the top section. I notice that the washing up bowl and other plastic items are bright orange; hardly tasteful but I suppose they are cheerful. Pinned to the wall is a calendar, with a young woman reclining seductively on a car bonnet, presumably a promotional gift from the local petrol station, proudly announcing in large letters MARCH 1970. If I had thought I could wish away this fact I was seriously mistaken.

The girls escort me to my room which is the other side of the hallway and it seems quite spacious. There is a fireplace which doesn't look as if it has ever been used, a wardrobe, a chest of drawers and a single bed. I half notice the sofa that my imposter mother disliked intensely but to be honest, I would not have chosen any of the furniture in the room.

All I really want to do is curl up in bed and hope this will turn out to be a horrible nightmare when I wake up but it seems a bit inappropriate to go to bed at five o'clock in the afternoon. In any case, it appears that Angie is cooking our favourite meal of "spag bol" for everyone this evening. I haven't a clue what it is.

I sit quietly in my room, thinking it all through. It seems my accident, whatever it was, has propelled me back into the past by some sixty years. I am still me, Jane Bonneville, and everyone seems to know me. In this life I seem to be a bit different. For example, I am supposed to be a teacher. Well, good luck with that Jane. I would really like to discuss this with someone but I am rather afraid they will think I am unhinged. In my real life I wouldn't hesitate to discuss the situation with my husband, my beloved Tom, but there is no one here I feel I could trust and I doubt Tom the cat would be of any use! I have not seen him yet but I hope he is a gentle cat, aside from the prolific mouse-catching which presumably serves a useful purpose. For the time being (oh dear, such phrases are meaningless at the moment), I will keep this strange and deeply worrying situation to myself.

I wander round the room, looking into drawers and the wardrobe. I find a dark blue British passport and notice that the photo – never flattering at the best of times – looks like me. There are a few other items that seem to confirm everything I have been told so far. I also have my hospital discharge papers from earlier today which show my date of birth, which was correct, except for the year. In my real life I was born on 2nd May 2000 and the form said 2nd May 1947. It gave my doctor's contact details which will be useful when I have the stitches removed from my forehead. I have a feeling that it will be a painful experience from what the nurse said. In my real life we use dissolvable thread and I don't think I have ever had stitches before, not even when I gave birth to the twins. At this thought my eyes fill with tears. I don't want to be here. I want to be in my own time with my family. I shake my head and try deep breathing to calm myself.

The contents of the wardrobe and chest of drawers were quite a shock and I wonder if I will feel remotely comfortable in those clothes. At a practical level, they will all need ironing and they all look so scruffy compared to my sleek and stylish everyday clothes in my real life.

'Grub's up,' called a distant voice so I leave the safety of my own room to see where the others are gathered for our meal.

Our shared dining room is also on the ground floor, in what we use in my real life as the boys' playroom. At this thought, tears threaten again but I manage to hold them at bay while the meal is discussed. "Spag bol" is apparently spaghetti bolognese which is minced beef in a tomato sauce served with pasta. It is highly regarded for being a foray into "foreign" food which I gather is fashionable now that people take holidays abroad. In any case, I quite enjoyed it, especially as our own range of foods has become so limited in recent years. There I go again, confusing my time with this time.

Angie had prepared the meal as it was known to be a favourite of mine, which was really thoughtful. I ate the meal with some gusto as I had not really eaten much while in hospital. Before I could thank Angie properly, she appeared with dessert. I have to be truthful, it was horrible. It was a sweet and sickly pink mousse called Angel Delight. Angie asked if I would like extras which I declined. 'To be honest, I prefer fresh fruit for afters,' I said. Everyone laughed but I was not sure why it was funny.

Having lost track of time (there I go again, using inappropriate phrases) I was not aware that tomorrow is Good Friday. This means everyone is at home and not at work. The girls suggested that I should take the day quietly and Sue offered to walk into Wimbledon with me for some window shopping if I felt like it. All the shops will be closed but it will help me re-orientate myself, according to Sue. I was grateful for the kind offer even though I wasn't sure why anyone would go shopping if the shops were all closed but it seemed a genuine suggestion so I accepted with alacrity.

'Oh, look at the time! We will miss Top of the Pops if we don't clear up quickly.' That said, everyone set to, taking the dishes into the kitchen and embarking on the washing up. It was strange. I'm not used to washing up by hand and drying everything with a tea towel.

The television was upstairs in a small spare room which otherwise functioned as a storage space. I stared at the small, wooden box with a tiny pale green screen which was perched on a small table. The picture, when it appeared, was extremely fuzzy and had really garish unnatural colours. I tried not to smile as I thought of our slimline flat screen equivalent with Smart technology and ultra-high definition, which masquerades as an aquarium of tropical fish when we are not watching something! Here we had to switch it on, wait until it warmed up and then change the channels by twiddling knobs. It's going to take me an awfully long time to get used to having no computer technology, I thought to myself.

Things got worse once the programme started. First there was an announcer who seemed to be dressed in clown's clothes. He had long white blonde hair and a strange wavering voice which did little to enhance the atmosphere. The first band started playing and they were called King Crimson. Well, what a noise! They were all in fancy dress too. After that was The Faces, much appreciated by my flatmates. I could not get over the clothes being worn by the audience nor the weird jigging up and down which passed for dancing. The commentary was fast, with a pseudo-American accent, which I could barely follow. A band called Pickettywitch was supposed to be playing but instead they had a lightly clad female dance troupe called Pan's People gyrating to the recorded music. The dancers were quite good but the dancing was explicit and no-one would tolerate that sort of thing now. Well, I mean in my own time.

Finally, it was over and everyone dispersed to their rooms. I went back to mine but felt completely at a loss to know what to do. In my real life, once the boys have gone to bed, I generally spend the rest of the evening talking with Tom or catching up with friends around the world via social media, listening to music, shopping or reading. Without my iPhone or access to the world wide web I just did not know what to do. I am also used to having a shower but there only seems to be a shared bath in the house at this time. Eventually I went to bed and slept fitfully, tortured by dreams of my lost life.

6. Settling In

The next morning, we all had breakfast at different times so I helped myself to cereal when I was ready. When Sue appeared, I asked her how we share the expenses. She explained that at the beginning of every month we have a "whip-round" for the rent and put money in the pot to pay for any meals we eat together, as well as for the gas and electricity bills. Angie manages all this. I'm finding it hard to grasp pounds, shillings and pence but it all seems very cheap. Sue also broke the news that it is my turn on the rota for today's meal. Thankfully she suggested we could buy fish and chips from the "chippy" as a treat and because it is Good Friday.

We agreed a time for going out for a walk around Wimbledon and I'm quite looking forward to seeing how much I recognise of my home town, even though it is years earlier than in my real life.

I also realise that I am still wearing the same jumper and skirt that Kate brought into the hospital for me. From a discreet observation of the others I suspect that the dress code for the holiday weekend at home seems to be jeans.

With a deep sigh I go through my wardrobe and find a tee-shirt and some trousers. The former was, I imagine, a cheap vest that has been subjected to tie-dyeing as it has swirls of blue and pink patterns all over it. I think it was a trend in this era. As for the trousers, I believe these are "bell bottoms" or maybe what they call "loons"? The fashions are confusing here. I try them on but they look dreadful with the platform shoes, in my opinion. That's annoying as I was just getting used to walking in them.

Exploring another cupboard, I find some more clothes which look marginally more acceptable to my eyes. There is a pair of navy Levi corduroy trousers and a multi-coloured top with zigzag patterns which is more suited to the cooler temperatures that we are experiencing today. Hidden by the bag that I tossed into the corner last night I find some gym shoes which I think will pass muster. I try all these on and apart from the afro hair-do I think I look OK.

One thing that really is bothering me is that I do not have my wedding ring. As far as I can tell, I was not wearing it in hospital and it was not with my purse which wasn't actually my purse, if you see what I mean. My left hand feels strangely bare and so often the other hand goes to the place where my ring should be. It is a constant reminder that I am not with Tom here in this place and time.

Sue tapped on the door at eleven-thirty and I noticed that she was wearing Levi's too which made me feel much better. As we walked slowly up the road – it is quite steep – Sue told me a little about each of the flatmates, including who was going out with who. Her boyfriend is called Pete and he's a P.E. teacher at a school in Putney. This gave me an opportunity to ask about the school where I was supposed to teach. I really haven't a clue how to deal with this problem but I'm hoping to be back in my own time before the new term begins. If not, I will think about it in a week or so and in the meantime, I am trying to put it to the back of my mind.

'You teach English at Ricards Lodge School. It's a girls' High School in Lake Road. We will be walking past it in a minute; maybe you will remember it when we do.'

I also discovered that Sue is a Primary School teacher, but I did not recognise the name of the school where she works as I think it is some distance away or maybe it does not exist in my time.

Kate works in a Pre-school Nursery and does not have a boyfriend at present. I am not sure quite what Sue is implying when she hesitates to explain this to me, so I just smile and nod.

Angie works in the head office of a retail shop called Marks & Spencer and is on a management training course. I do not know much about this company as I believe it closed down round about the time the twins were born but of course I nod my head as if I am familiar with it. Angie's boyfriend is a car mechanic in a large garage in Croydon.

By this stage of our walk we are close to the school and I look blankly at the gates which are currently chained up because of the Easter holidays. 'I'm sorry Sue but I do not recognise anything. I really don't know what I am going to do when I have to go back to work.'

Sue reassures me that things will come back gradually and I should not worry.

We stroll onwards to Wimbledon High Street and along its length I see some buildings that I recognise: first the Library, then the station, Elys department store and at the far end there is Wimbledon Theatre. There are others that I do not know: a Wimpey bar, which is a fast food outlet and numerous shops such as Boots, WH Smith, Timothy Whites, Woolworths etc which do not exist in my time. I continue to feel dreadfully dislocated.

Sue suggested we could come out again tomorrow if there is anything I want to buy at the shops.

We stroll back to the flat, talking very little but in companionable silence.

As soon as we are in the door, Angie bounds down the stairs. 'Jane, you have just missed a phone call from your mum. They were wanting to know how you were coping.'

'What did you tell her, Angie?'

'To be honest I did not really have a chance to say anything.'

'Why doesn't that surprise me,' I laughed, feeling more at home amongst my new friends than I had expected.

'I have a confession to make, though' she grimaced, 'I have invited your parents to Sunday lunch. I thought they could see for themselves that you are doing OK. Also, your mum said she had some things for you.'

I looked from Angie to Sue to see how they reacted to the prospect of sharing Sunday lunch with my imposter family. 'That's fine by me as I'll be at Pete's on Sunday,' said Sue.

'I will be around and so will Kate,' said Angie. 'I thought we could have a nice roast chicken and all the trimmings.' I was already beginning to experience Angie's organisational skills!

'Speaking of food, when should I get tonight's fish and chips?' I asked. We agreed it was a little early but at that moment Kate emerged from the bathroom and volunteered to go with me later.

As it happens, I think I already know the fish and chip shop, if it is in the same place as the one in my real life. All the same, I thought it would be good to have Kate with me as I am finding pre-decimal money a bit confusing. Not only do the coins look different, it is hard not to automatically think of everything in tens. I am so used to cashless transactions I'm bound to drop the coins in the fish fryer or something!

I sat down in my room while I was waiting and very quietly a large black cat wandered in. He seemed to take control of the situation by jumping up and making himself at home on my lap. This, of course, is Tom. He has a very loud purr which gets amplified once he starts washing. A steady lick, lick, lick is really sleep inducing and I start to relax totally.

Of course, I cannot help thinking about the real Tom. When I close my eyes it's almost as if he is with me in this strange time. Tom is quite tall. Well, he's taller than me. He has dark brown hair which is cut fairly short except for the floppy bit at the front. He has crinkles round his eyes when he smiles, which isn't very often because he's quite serious and thoughtful. When he does smile his whole face lights up.

His very dark brown eyes are framed by gorgeous eyelashes that many women would die for. He has what I think is called a "Roman" nose which makes him look very distinguished. His lips, well, what can I say? I just wish he was here with me now as I would be testing those lips to destruction! I could tell you about the rest of his body but that would be rude, so I'd better not. Oh Tom… whatever has happened to me? I really want to get home right now.

Kate taps on the door shortly and I find that over an hour has passed since our earlier conversation. 'I knew he would be happy once you were home,' she said, pointing at Tom who was still fast asleep on my lap. 'Well he certainly got me to relax too!' I replied.

We strolled slowly along to the chip shop while Kate told me a little about her work. I like Kate. She is very easy to be with. As we approached, I was pleased to see that I could recognise the chip shop which has changed really very little. It was being run by a Polish couple who seemed to know Kate and in fact, the woman smiled at me as if she knew me too. 'Haddock and chips four times, please' said Kate. I was astounded how inexpensive it was and the fish looked to be of good quality too. In my own time fresh fish is very hard to come by except in top level restaurants. I think it is something to do with depleted fish stocks in the North Sea as well as the economic situation. Tom and I very rarely use the chippy and if we do, we tend to have one of the vegetarian options.

This life is so very different and I miss my family dreadfully but for the time being I find I do like my flatmates. Sharing a flat with three girls is almost like being a student.

I hope I will be able to cope with my new situation until I can discover how get back to the twenty-first century.

7. Not in a Happy Place

The fish and chip supper was fine and I really did think I was beginning to accommodate to my situation. The rest of the evening was, unfortunately, a proper wake-up call.

Angie, in organisational mode, suggested we could go out to the pub for a relaxing drink as it was Friday night. Everyone else agreed, so it was expected I would go too. While I washed up the used plates it would seem everyone else went to their rooms to get dressed. I did not change from my jeans because I don't really like anything else in the wardrobe and I had been hoping I could buy some clothes more to my taste next week. I'm used to wearing designer sportswear when I am not at work, although that concept doesn't seem to be in fashion in 1970. The others all emerged in maxi skirts and winter coats.

Kate wore an Astrakhan coat (which I thought only old ladies used to wear!), Sue's coat was an attractive heavily embroidered velvet and Angie was trying to decide whether it was too mild to wear her Afghan coat. Eventually she decided on another, which I'm guessing was a second-hand animal fur. I cringe to think how the animal rights activists in my real life would react to that. 'Did you want to change, Jane?' asked Angie. It seemed like a subtle hint but I chose to ignore it. 'No, I'm fine thanks.'

We set off towards the Rose and Crown which is in Wimbledon Village. 'Let's have a kitty for the drinks,' suggested Angie. I opened the purse that the hospital had insisted was mine, and realised that the few coins therein probably did not amount to much. I mentioned this to the others and asked if there was a cash machine nearby. They looked a bit puzzled then Sue remembered seeing an item on the news which was announcing the first automated teller machine. It is in North

London but no one thought it was available south of the Thames yet. Sue offered to lend me some money until I could get to the bank after the Bank Holiday. I have to be much more careful about assuming that everything we have in my real life is here too. I don't think anyone noticed too much.

There was some talk of writing a cheque which filled me with horror. Cheques are never used in my own time as we function almost exclusively on a cashless basis, mainly using contactless payments. It occurs to me that cashing a cheque could be difficult as I don't know what the signature of the twentieth century me looks like. Also, I have no idea how much is in the bank account. In fact, I don't even know which is my bank.

Before I had time to worry about all that, we arrived at the pub. I can barely describe the shock I received as we went in. Across the room there was such a thick pall of smoke it was almost impossible to see the bar. It seemed that everyone was smoking cigarettes. My eyes began to stream with tears and I started choking. I had to go outside straight away. Kate followed me out. 'Are you OK Jane? Did something upset you?' she asked sympathetically. I took several lungsful of fresh air as I started to make sense of this. Clearly, in 1970 no one worried about the health warnings associated with smoking and unlike in my own time, the habit was not banned from public places. Now how do I handle this? 'Oh, I am sorry Kate. I am still finding my amnesia a bit of a problem,' I lied. 'It is a bit like claustrophobia as I feel uncomfortable in confined spaces.' I was almost beginning to believe this version of events myself.

'Let's go and sit in the beer garden for a while, until you feel better.'

I would have enjoyed a small glass of white wine but that did not seem to fit with what the others were drinking so I accepted a pint of bitter. The local brewery, Youngs, was apparently well thought-of, although I tried not to think about the polluted water in the nearby river Wandle going into their premium beer. Maybe the river was clean in 1970.

Two pints later and still in the garden, I started to relax. Kate had discreetly explained my ostensible reason for sitting outside and Sue and Angie had considerately come out to sit with us.

The conversation turned to holidays. Angie was talking about what she and Rob planned to do in the summer. Sue and Pete, both being teachers, had some six weeks to fill and were planning to go to Cornwall. Kate was rather quiet until Angie asked her what she had in mind. 'Will you be going away with your friend?' Kate blushed and said she did not know yet. There was an ominous silence which was quite a puzzle to me. Sensing some discomfort, I said I had not thought about it yet either. All three turned and with one voice chorused, 'Jane, you must remember! You've been saving for months to go to Toronto to see your aunt and uncle.'

Here we go again, I thought. How can I know things that have not happened to me? The Jane they think is their flatmate is not me. I didn't know I was supposed to have an aunt and uncle in Canada. This is all too difficult. It is impossible for me to pretend any more. I'm the imposter, not those kind people who are supposed to be my parents. As I opened my mouth to begin to say something, I realised that my situation defied explanation.

'Hello ladies, are you looking for a good time?' This from a fairly unappealing and scarcely articulate young man who, from his demeanour, had presumably been in the pub since opening time. My flatmates all looked in the other direction but somehow, because my mouth was preparing to speak, some unplanned words came out: 'We are having a good time already thanks. We certainly don't need your assistance.'

'Ooooh,' he replied. 'What a load of lesbians. We don't need you either. Come on,' he said to his mates, 'let's do a bit of queer-bashing on the Common.'

I was appalled on so many levels and was tempted to go after him to try to explain why he was so wrong but Angie, very sensibly, suggested we finished our drinks and made our way home.

On the walk back, I said to Kate that I thought we should call the police as what they were going to do was surely against the law. I was furious that no one else in the pub garden saw fit to remonstrate with them. I mentioned LGBT rights but that didn't seem to be a term she was familiar with, which reminded me again that these were different times to my own. She said that only last year a young homosexual man was murdered nearby on Clapham Common. Her quiet words suddenly put things into perspective for me. 'Thank you, Jane. I know you understand but a lot of people don't and I just have to be careful.'

After that, I really did not want to make the effort to talk to my flatmates. I want to scream, 'I shouldn't be here. Take me home to my husband and children. I hate this place.' Instead, after a quick mug of coffee purely to be sociable I said I was tired and went to my room. I cannot stop crying. My heart aches for Tom and the boys and my comfortable real life.

8. Starting My Diary

After breakfast, Sue and I reprised our walk into town, taking a slightly different route so I could build up a picture of my environment. Of course, I cannot tell her that I am familiar with Wimbledon in the twenty-first century and in any case, there have been so many changes I can barely recognise my home town.

Sue asked if I wanted to buy anything. I had thought about this last night and said I could do with a hair brush. 'You know what I think?' she suggested. 'You need a proper comb for your afro hair-do; let's go into Boots and see if they have one.' Of course, they did and it gave me a chance to use this pre-decimalisation money in the purse I had brought with me from the hospital. All went well and I agreed the new comb would be just right.

We called into WH Smith, a stationery shop, as Sue needed some envelopes. This is quite strange for me as I'm used to buying pretty much everything on line and in any case I contact people by text or email, writing by hand on paper is very rare. It did, however, give me an idea. I seem to remember that there is a therapeutic approach when people are feeling distressed which involves writing a diary. Maybe this is what I can do to help me make some sense of what has happened to me? I found a notebook with colourful psychedelic pictures on the cover and purchased this, as well as a biro. It's so funny. It almost feels like I am on holiday in a strange country.

After we had done our personal shopping, we bought the food for the parental lunch tomorrow. The idea of needing to find time to fit in the task of buying food is gradually sinking in. I am so used to ordering on line and having a once a week delivery to the house.

Saturday afternoon was taken up with housework. Angie directed operations, as usual. While Kate and I cleaned downstairs and our own rooms, Sue and Angie did upstairs. It took a long time as we had to take turns and everything had to be done with a really cumbersome vacuum cleaner which had to be moved between (in)accessible electric sockets! It was strange for me as I am used to my home robot doing these things. In my own time all I have to do is tidy each room and empty the i-vac dust box.

That evening the four of us watched television but I did not enjoy it. Actually, I was shocked and appalled. It was dreadful. We watched a programme called "Til Death Us Do Part". The main character was called Alf Garnett who was a racist bigot. I was not comfortable watching it. It was meant to be a comedy but it wasn't funny. The other characters were almost as bad but they did nothing to challenge the attitudes of Alf. I went to bed after starting my diary.

Saturday March 28th
My name is Jane Bonneville and I am married to Tom. We have two lovely children Logan and Theo. I was on my way to work when something strange happened and I am now living in 1970. In my real life it is 2027. I want to go home but I don't know how. The people in my new life are kind and they all think they know me. Apart from missing my family, which is the worst thing ever, I hate not having access to the internet. I didn't realise what a fundamental part of my life it is. I am so lonely and I don't know what to do.

That was all I wrote but I thought it was a start and would give me something to focus on, a bit like having an imaginary friend! It moved me no further towards a solution though.

During the night I woke up with a good idea. I might not be able to use Google or Wikipedia etc but I could do what people used to do before the internet existed and that was to go to the library. For a start, I could search for some information about amnesia so I can make sure I am behaving correctly. I was so encouraged I made a note in my diary.

Action
Go to Wimbledon Library and research i) amnesia and ii) time travel and parallel lives?

9. Plan of Action

On Sunday morning I woke up feeling almost enthusiastic for the day ahead. I know that I will have a lot of difficulties while I am here because everything is so different but if I'm careful and methodical I may be able to find a way out of the situation I find myself in.

I am trying hard not to think of Logan and Theo and the Easter egg hunt we had planned for today. I really cannot imagine if I am absent from my own time or if there is another Jane who has taken my place. Sometimes I could scream with frustration and if not that, I cry my eyes out. Mostly I cry quietly alone in my room so I've managed not to let the others know I'm so desperately unhappy.

Under the circumstances, the day was quite a success. There was a lot of preparation for lunch and it took time because there are none of the labour-saving devices here that I take for granted in my real life. Everything has to be peeled and washed and prepared by hand. Washing up the dishes is deeply tedious. Who would have thought I would crave my dishwasher? Usually I barely give the machine a thought.

My imposter Mum and Dad arrived mid-morning and sat chatting with Angie while Kate and I cooked. Mum had brought two bags of things from my bedroom at home. These included old birthday cards and quite a few documents that she had taken out of the little desk in the bedroom. I probably did not need the doll and the teddy bear but I'm sure she was trying to be helpful by offering some items that would trigger recollections. Of course, I knew they wouldn't as it wasn't me that grew up with them but it was thoughtful of her. I managed to avoid any major faux pas by keeping fairly quiet.

After they had left, I looked at everything and familiarised myself with the person they think I am. It's very uncomfortable. I imagine it is rather like an actress taking on a new role but I just wish I could be myself.

The next day, everyone else was busy, so I took myself off for a stroll on Wimbledon Common. It was quite relaxing as the sun was shining and it was dry underfoot. I walked as far as the Windmill where I sat for a while watching families enjoying themselves until I felt so homesick that I had to leave. The walk gave me an opportunity to reflect on what had happened to me and to ponder what I should do next.

I realise that feeling miserable and powerless isn't getting me anywhere nor is it doing me any good. I need to take advantage of this strange situation while getting on with finding out how to get back to my real life. Back in my room, I made a note in my diary as my plan of action.

Monday March 30th
Had a lovely walk on Wimbledon Common, although it added to my feelings of homesickness.

Action
This week I will:
i) check out where my GP's surgery is and make the appointment to have my stitches removed
ii) have another look at the school where I'm supposed to be a teacher
iii) go to the library to research what could have happened to me
iv) go to the bank and find out how much money I have
v) buy some new clothes!

That seemed like quite enough to be going on with and although I had actually achieved nothing it felt as if I was facing up to my problems and doing my best to manage the situation.

I did go to the library and although it was, overall, a disappointment I did at least manage to find some information about amnesia.

In my own time, the library in Wimbledon is a beautiful, old red brick building which is used for many purposes. We have a deli, an internet café and a meeting place for young mothers. It is also where my office is based.

I was quite realistic about what I would find today but it was still a shock to find there was nothing but books, books, books and more books. I went to the reference section and eventually discovered a medical encyclopaedia. The entry on amnesia, which I copied by hand into my notebook, was as follows:

Amnesia is a deficit in memory caused by brain damage, disease, or psychological trauma. The memory can be either wholly or partially lost due to the extent of damage that was caused. There are two main types of amnesia: retrograde amnesia and anterograde amnesia. Retrograde amnesia is the inability to retrieve information that was acquired before a particular date, usually the date of an accident or operation. In some cases, the memory loss can extend back decades, while in others the person may lose only a few months of memory.

There was a lot of information about all the different types of amnesia and an explanation about treatment. The bit I found most useful was discovering that many forms of amnesia fix themselves without being treated.

Of course, I gave all of this much thought, because it is possible that I actually do have amnesia as a result of an accident and all my memories of Tom and the boys and my life in 2027 is in my imagination. I'm not confident of that theory though.

I risked watching the TV this week with my flatmates. We saw a special edition of Dixon of Dock Green, a rather gentle police drama. It was quite relaxing but I did find it amusing privately that policemen just had whistles to communicate with each other and merely a wooden truncheon to deal with miscreants when threatened. No mobile phones, bodycams or tasers here then.

I have achieved quite a lot from my action list. The GP was pleasant and she chatted to me while she removed my stitches. This hurt quite a bit more than I expected but although there is an angry-looking scar it will not draw attention to my face as much as those black stitches did. The bruises are slowly fading to a rather nasty purple and yellow but they will go in due course. The doctor was very kind and asked me how I felt in general as well as checking whether any cognitive function had returned. I said that it had not and that I was worried about going back to work. She suggested I should give it a try and if it was too difficult, she would give me a sick note for my employer.

I did go back to have a look at Ricards Lodge School as per my action list but apart from discovering the name of the headmistress from the noticeboard I was no nearer to knowing how to deal with my teaching commitments.

I entertained myself by making a second visit to Wimbledon library; this was almost as pointless as the first time. I had not realised how boring and time-consuming it is to have to hunt for information. My goodness, this experience is making me realise how valuable a good search engine is. All I could discover on the subject of parallel lives, alternative universes, time travel and things like that was that they only exist in the shelves of science fiction books. There is absolutely nothing of any help to someone like myself who is in the throes of an unplanned and unexplained adventure in another time frame.

As it turned out, I didn't have any trouble at the bank. I had found a cheque book in my room and so I knew that the other me banked at Barclays. Yes, I know that sounds rather schizophrenic but it is confusing differentiating between the real me and the one I am having to live with at the moment.

I was quite nervous about going in to the bank because in my own time we don't have banks in buildings as they are all on line. The teller at the bank was happy to print out a bank statement for my current account once I showed her my passport as identification. Thankfully, the account was in credit so I withdrew £100. I had real qualms about my signature being recognised but I need not have worried; I just did my usual squiggle and the cash was handed over. She asked me if I was buying something very special and I realised that people tended not to walk around with that amount of cash in their wallets in 1970!

I did pay a visit to Elys which is a department store but I could not find any clothes that I liked, so my cash is untouched for now.

Every day, I try to keep my feelings hidden from my flatmates but once I am alone in my room, the tears of distress and frustration overwhelm me. I do not want to be here although I am trying to cope as well as possible so that I can find my way home to my loved ones.

I am no stranger to loss and bereavement and I thought I had grown stronger as a result, but this situation is completely new. I feel like a child again with no one to turn to for help.

I'm sure all the other mums at Logan and Theo's school think I am a very ordinary wife and mother, but I bet none of them grew up experiencing the roller-coaster of a life that I did. I won't bore you with the gory details right now but imagine the seven-year-old me coming home from school to find that the two people I loved the most in all the world were dead. My mum and dad both died in a tragic car accident. They were on the way to the dentist and a couple of boy racers smashed into them in a stolen car. They died instantly.

Suddenly I was uprooted from my quiet rural junior school by my grandparents and plunged into the centre of London. Of course, they did their best for me but they had their own lives and a little, grieving girl did not fit into it well.

Nan and Grandad became the parents I didn't have any more. I even called them Mum and Dad because it saved having to explain to school friends and their parents what had happened.

I suppose, as a result, I have always been fairly self-sufficient and very focussed on ensuring that our home was stable and loving for the boys.

Anyway, here I am again, plunged into a strange world that I do not want to be part of and just longing for everything to go back to the way it was.

10. Back to School

I have been talking with my flatmate Sue about returning to teaching next week. Of course, I have not told her that I have had no training whatsoever nor that I have never taught in my life. I thought I might pick up a few clues from her but I now realise after our conversation that there is a big difference between a Primary School, where she teaches, and the Girls' School where I am supposed to work.

Sue understands that I still have a complete blank in my memory of the last ten or more years so she was very helpful in 'reminding' me of things I could have forgotten. I confessed I did not even know what to wear and she kindly went through my wardrobe and picked out a few suitable items. She seemed to think that a rather horrible (in my opinion) pale blue suit, which looks home-made, would be ideal for the first day back. So I can add that to all the other reasons why I will feel stressed and deeply uncomfortable.

Apparently, the summer term begins a couple of days later for her, whereas in my school there is a staggered return with the older girls beginning on Thursday and the rest of the school on Friday, ready for 'business as usual' the next Monday.

Thursday April 9th
To be honest I am really terrified about going 'back to work' but I cannot avoid it. I will just have to grit my teeth and put on a brave face. I have also been thinking about what is happening in my real world. Is there another Jane there who has taken my place, feeding my children and sleeping with my husband? Much as I try not to keep worrying, I am still wide awake and it is four o'clock in the morning.

I am not sure the diary is really helping me as I end up writing down all my worries and fears which go around and round in my head at night.

I've had a quick breakfast of cereal, combed the dreaded Afro hair and checked my appearance numerous times. I have also had a serious word with myself along the lines of 'they are only children, Jane – how awful can they be?'

The walk to school takes about ten minutes and this time the gates are open. As I approach, a girl in bottle green school uniform rushes up to me, 'Miss Bonneville! How are you? Are you better after your accident?'

'Much improved, thank you but not quite my old self yet,' I reply, having rehearsed this sentence several times during the night. Deep breath. Try to sound casual, Jane. 'Oh, could you point me in the direction of my classroom?'

The helpful pupil takes me in through the main door, and as we pass along the corridor I notice 'Mrs Staples Headmistress' on one door, next to the similarly labelled 'Staff Room'. After striding along several more corridors I am delivered to my classroom. I thank the girl without discovering her name and rush in, closing the door firmly behind me.

I spend a few minutes familiarising myself with the room, which has thirty-eight desks in it, a large roller blackboard and a cupboard at the front behind the teacher's desk. I don't know why I had not anticipated a blackboard but it was a shock. Foolishly I had pictured a laptop on the desk and an integrated screen on the wall behind. How am I going to write with chalk?

Before I had time to figure this out, a bell rang and gradually the girls began to enliven the classroom with their chatter. I waited until it seemed that most of the desks were filled, responding to enquiries about my recovery from the accident in vague terms, then I tapped on the desk. Immediately everyone went quiet. If any of them had been very observant, they would have seen my hands trembling with nerves. 'Good morning, everyone,' I began and as I opened my mouth to speak again the class chorused as with one voice, 'Good morning, Miss Bonneville.' I wasn't expecting that!

Then another girl entered the room and handed me the class register. I had a rough idea that it was to record who was there but that was about all I could recall from my own school days.

I opened the large foolscap folder and saw that someone had helpfully ruled a line for the morning's attendance and headed it 9/4/70. As if it was the most natural thing in the world, I began to read out loud the names going down the list and marked with a tick everyone who responded, 'Yes, Miss.' When finished, I flicked back a page and realised that I should have made a forward slash not a tick. Oh well, too late to worry about that now. The girls had started to talk again, presumably comparing notes about their Easter break. Just as I was wondering how to proceed, another girl came in to collect the register and a bell rang again. This time the girls took exercise books out of their desks and headed for the door. Panic set in. What shall I do now?

Before I had time to react, another group of girls came in the room. They seemed about the same age as the last lot and when I looked more carefully, I could see that some of the original group whose attendance I had recorded, were still here.

I turned to the cupboard behind my desk for inspiration. The shelves were full of novels and English exercise books. Pinned inside the door was a timetable which informed me that as it was Thursday, 5G were currently in my presence. There were also some postcards presumably collected from an art gallery somewhere, including the famous painting of Ophelia by Millais. While the subject matter was dreadfully sad, I was pleased that the Miss Bonneville who was usually here had good taste. She also had a sense of humour as there was another picture showing twenty cats' facial expressions, all identical, but labelled individually 'happy, sad, thoughtful, hungry, cross, naughty' etc.

I turned back to the class and asked what they had done in the last English class before the holiday. 'We had a supply teacher Miss, and she gave us a comprehension exercise.' Having ascertained that they all had the correct book with them, but had not finished the task owing to a certain amount of jollity just before breaking up for Easter, I suggested that they should take twenty minutes to finish the piece and then we would mark it together. Clever, eh? That will save me having to mark it myself.

While they were working, fairly quietly I have to say, I read the text and made a rough note of the correct answers. I am beginning to think I could make a go of this teaching lark. After twenty minutes they begged for a little more time, so I waited until it seemed that everyone had finished.

Suddenly I realised that it was going to be difficult as I did not know anyone's name. Pointing seemed rude, especially as I had presumably been teaching this group for at least two thirds of a year. 'Who thinks they have the correct answer to question one?' Several hands went up and I had to resort to pointing.

Unfortunately, the girl I selected was the class clown and she gave what was obviously a silly answer. Everyone laughed and someone said, 'Oh Miss, fancy asking Vanessa, she never knows.' I ploughed on in this vein for several minutes until the aforementioned Vanessa called out 'Miss doesn't know any of us. She's forgotten our names!' There was much laughter and I really wished the floor would open up and swallow me. I explained that after a serious head injury people can have a little memory loss but that I would soon get it back.

Somehow, I kept going until the bell rang. I wanted to run away and cry but before I could decide what to do, 5G filed out and another batch of young women came in.

This group seemed less amenable and I could see I was going to have trouble with them. For a start, they did not go quiet when I tapped the desk. I was about to raise my voice when a fight started towards the back of the room. I could see nails clawing at faces, long hair being flayed around while chairs and desks crashed to the floor and other members of the class shouted, quite unnecessarily I thought, 'Fight! Fight! Fight!'

Quickly I dashed to where the action was happening and with some difficulty prised the two girls apart. 'That's enough,' I cried, shaking with distress. I had no idea who started it or what the fight was about. Nor did I have any idea how to deal with it. 'Send them to Miss Staples, Miss,' shouted one girl helpfully. Thinking quickly, I said, 'No. They can prove they can act their age by sitting down quietly for the rest of the lesson.' I pointed to an empty desk at the front of the room and indicated that one of them should sit there, so that they were separated. Once the upended desks were put back and the antagonists were calmed down I decided that trying the same tactic with this class as I had used with 5G, would be unwise.

'What was the last book we were reading? Can anyone remember?' It seemed that that it was 'My Family and Other Animals' by Gerald Durrell, the naturalist. Thankfully, a version of this story had been filmed for television in my own time and I had watched a couple of episodes. 'Oh Miss, will you read it to us and do the funny voices like you always do?' Together we found roughly where to continue and for the next thirty-five minutes I read with as many funny voices as I could muster.

The bell for lunch break rang and I breathed a sigh of utter relief. It was obvious to me that I was totally ill-equipped for this job. I walked down the corridor and knocked on the door of the headmistress's office. By that stage my face was wet with tears. Mrs Staples opened the door and gestured for me to come in.

'Jane. Are you alright? I wondered why we didn't see you in the staffroom.' Her kind and gentle tone only served to open the floodgates and I sobbed almost uncontrollably. Eventually I dried my eyes and explained how very difficult it was for me when I didn't remember any names or anything about how to teach. It was hard to tell her that my mind was a blank but I had to offer at least that level of honesty. 'What do you want to do?' she said.

'The truth is, I don't think I will ever be able to go back to what I used to do. I would prefer to resign and give the school a chance to replace me so that the pupils do not suffer in their examinations.'

Mrs Staples spent several minutes trying to convince me to give it another go but my mind was made up. We agreed in the end that I would get a sick note from my GP and if after a couple of weeks, I was still of the same opinion, she would accept my resignation.

'Go home now and I will sort out a supply teacher for the time being,' she suggested. 'Do you want to say hello to your colleagues?' Of course, that would have been horrendous as I do not know any of them so I declined, collected my jacket and left as quickly as possible.

Somehow, the afternoon passed with me alternately sitting in my room or lurking in the kitchen making mugs of tea for myself.

Sue was the first to arrive home and one glance at my face told its story. She hugged me, listened to my tale of woe and actually agreed that I had probably taken the best course of action. 'There's no point in prolonging the misery. You can get yourself a bit better then look for another job, something different.'

When Kate and Angie arrived, they too listened sympathetically and supported my decision. Then Angie unintentionally provided the killer punch, 'When will you tell your parents? They are sure to be disappointed.' That set me off crying again. Of course, she was right. Everything I had seen so far suggested that they placed great store on being able to tell people, 'our daughter is a teacher'. We agreed there would be no need to tell them yet, so if they phoned and one of the others answered the call they would not say anything.

I may be in an awful situation, most of which my flatmates are entirely unaware, but at least they were kind and supportive.

I didn't feel like eating but they insisted I had a small portion of cottage pie that Kate had prepared the day before. Frankly, I was sick and tired of meals made from minced beef but it did seem to be the main source of protein. I ate it with good grace and volunteered to prepare tomorrow's meal – not fish and chips this time – as I would have the day to myself once they had all gone to work.

11. What Next?

Remarkably, I slept well last night. I suppose it was because I was exhausted with the stress of the previous day as well as feeling relieved that I did not have to go back to school. After breakfast I phoned the doctor's surgery to make an appointment in order to get a sick note. I have not yet really got used to the dreadfully cumbersome telephone handset and the need to rotary dial a number, wait for the correct tone and then push my coins into the slot. I was amazed to be offered an appointment at the end of the afternoon. In my real life, there is often a two week wait to see a doctor in person although we can use the virtual doctor which is cheaper. The concept is fine but not much use if you need tests or if the GP needs to see you in person to assess your condition.

I thought I would go out first thing to do the food shopping. There is a small supermarket in town, obviously a forerunner to the extensive food halls we had in the noughties, before many of our hypermarkets closed following the proliferation of on-line shopping and home delivery. I suspect the economic situation has affected what we can buy too. We have probably accepted the fact that the range and quality of produce has reduced in recent years and it's not obvious if you don't actually walk round a supermarket at all. I have, in any case, only ever in my real life bought my shopping online with a weekly delivery. Ticking off the items one wants from the list presented on the screen means that you take what's on offer without coming up with more imaginative alternatives.

This wasn't my first trip to the little supermarket in Wimbledon in 1970 as I had been there earlier with my flatmate Sue to get the shopping for the Easter Sunday meal with my parents. This time I was hoping to find some seafood and the ingredients for Mediterranean roast vegetables. The first thing I noticed was that there was no garlic and the selection of vegetables was quite limited. I was getting used to everything being comparatively inexpensive, so I was not prepared for the exorbitant price of the olive oil. I decided I would be able to roast the vegetables but it would not be the same as in my real life. The search for some seafood proved fruitless too. There were a few items of frozen food, mainly peas but not the prawns I was looking for. In the end, I selected some chicken pieces and some jars of spices which would liven it up.

While I was in town I walked to the end of the shops towards the theatre. The posters outside showed that Cinderella had been the pantomime this winter but there did not seem to be any plays currently showing.

A little further on, were some offices. I am not really familiar with this end of town in my real life as the twins' school, the station and my office are nearer to Wimbledon village. There was quite a scruffy café which I decided to venture into as I was feeling quite weary and needed a break before heading back to the flat.

I sipped my coffee and reflected on my strange life. At the moment, I cannot see any way that I can get back to my own time. I push those thoughts away, not wanting to cry in public.

As I left the café, I noticed a postcard in the window. It was advertising a vacancy for a secretary in the trade union office next door. Anyway, it's time I was getting back to the flat with this heavy bag of shopping to prepare our meal.

The evening's meal was much appreciated and the girls thought it was quite exotic. Overall it has not been a bad day. I enjoyed wandering around the town, looking at buildings I recognised and many that have since been demolished. The GP was happy to give me a sick note which stated that I would not be able to work in my current employment for an indefinite period. That really indicated the end of my short-lived teaching career.

I have been thinking a lot about work. Although I have one month's salary in hand in my bank account, it will be necessary for me to find another job soon. I am wondering about that secretarial job. Like everyone else I have keyboard skills and my real-life job in recruitment might give me some insights into how trade unions work. Of course, in my own time the unions have little power although they still exist in some industries. I might check out the vacancy next week.

Friday April 10th
Mum phoned earlier this evening. Apparently, my aunt in Toronto has passed away unexpectedly. While I was suitably sympathetic (well done Jane, especially given that I don't know her) I was delighted that she thought it would not be possible for me to visit uncle this summer as he has gone to stay with family some miles away. She was so full of this news there was no opportunity to tell her that I have been back at work for one day and that I have handed in my notice. In fact, I had to stop her flow of conversation to say that I needed to finish eating my dinner!

12. My View of the Wider World

This morning everyone was up for breakfast at around the same time which was lovely. Angie was reading her newspaper and every few moments she was conveying the main facts for the rest of us to discuss.

It strikes me that the world of 1970 is a much more optimistic and, in some ways, a gentler period than my own time, although of course I could not share any of these reflections with my flatmates.

For example, here they watch the BBC news daily and regularly listen to the World Service on a radio. There's a large number of printed daily newspapers both national and local which range through serious news issues to informed presentation, popular culture, contemporary events and satirical writing or light-hearted gossip. No one questions the facts that are presented or the information given, even though much of the media is state sponsored.

In my own time we only read news on-line and we rely mainly on selected social media to be accurate in the first place or to provide evidence to challenge fake news when necessary. Very little government sponsored media is recognised; we know it is heavily funded by party donors and therefore biased. There are a few print papers left but these are usually cheap advertising circulars.

Here, we have a General Election coming up in June. The daily papers, depending on their political stance, are highlighting the achievements of the Labour government under Prime Minister Harold Wilson or contrasting what the Conservatives will do, with Edward Heath at the helm. It will be a landmark election as 18-year olds will be able to vote for the first time.

To date it looks as if the Labour government will win another term in office. I wonder privately if I will still be stuck here in June or whether I will have found my way back to my own time before then.

Whatever the outcome here, people do seem to be full of hope. Contrast that with my own time where most of us are deeply cynical about politicians and the system of administration. There is little trust between people and consequently alarming levels of "petty" crime, poor mental health and suicide.

In the late 2020s we are still getting over major schisms in society, not just in the UK as a result of an ill-conceived referendum but across all major industrialised countries. The problems have included religious differences, in-fighting within the main political parties, constitutional crises as well as being a very difficult period for global economies.

In addition, for several years, we have been wrangling over how to modify the detailed elements of our daily lives in relation to climate change. Fuel shortages have largely been resolved by a major shift to electric powered vehicles, for those who can afford them. The impact on many industries is still being felt. Many people have been displaced from their country of birth as a result of food shortages and the refugee crisis caused by political and religious difference is far from being resolved. Immigration policy in the UK has been softened somewhat but I don't think anyone realised quite how severely the exodus of EU nationals would impact on the economy. The threat of losing the ability to learn, live, love and work in the rest of Europe meant that individuals had to make some heart-breaking decisions such as whether to stay with a husband and children or whether to return to their birth country to care for elderly parents. No wonder 1970 seems a much gentler time to me.

I noticed when I was food shopping yesterday that, although there are some items not available, the shelves are much better stocked than in my own time. Either that or my delivery company is not telling me the truth when we have shortages! I think my flatmates would be shocked to know about the levels of food poverty we have in 2027. Fresh fruit and vegetables are a luxury and food substitutes are widespread. They are being marketed as ecologically sound i.e. kind to animals and providing a reduction in our carbon footprint but personally I don't enjoy the artificial taste of the plant-based meat substitutes grown in laboratories across the country.

There are some things that are similar though. Inflation is high here and there is an undercurrent of strikes and industrial troubles. It doesn't seem anything like as bad as in my own time where we have regular outbreaks of civil unrest. Sadly, homelessness has increased and crime levels have risen considerably. With reductions in the numbers of police and armed forces, food riots are difficult to keep under control.

Angie's newspaper makes much of the problems of the NHS today and it is hard for me to restrain myself from telling them how wonderful it is. After my recent experience of healthcare in 1970 both in hospital and the GP service, I can assure them it is far superior to the commercial, competitive system we now have. For us, the insurance costs are too great for all but the wealthiest people. The mantra of "free at the point of delivery" has all but gone.

I did wonder whether I should be claiming for my injury from the bus company (not that I'm actually aware of any details of my supposed accident), which would be normal in my own time but when I tentatively mentioned it the other day everyone seemed to be outraged. It seems that in the USA they have a "compensation culture" and that "everyone" is litigious but we don't do that in the UK and it is not needed because we have the NHS. I thought it best not to mention it again!

Of course, in my own time we do have much to be proud of. Public Health campaigns and government action has reduced drug and alcohol consumption, aided by rising costs I suppose, and smoking in public places has been banned for years. Compared with my own time I am also very aware, while I am living in 1970, that racism and sexism are still deeply embedded in people's attitudes. Those things are reinforced here by news items and television, even entertainment.

Eventually everyone leaves the breakfast table and I realise that the discussion was partly for my benefit as my thoughtful flatmates are trying to help me recover my memory. They are kind and I certainly could have landed in a much less safe place than here.

13. Job Hunting

Although I have been signed off by the doctor for another week and will receive my teacher's pay until the end of the month, I think I should begin to look for a job. I certainly cannot live in the 20th century without any money.

The advert for a secretary that I saw in the café near the theatre last week seems a good place to start. I presume that they will want a CV or at the very least an application form. In my real life I would just review the basic CV I have already saved on my laptop, modify it to suit the specific vacancy, print off a copy for reference, then email the tailored document with a covering letter to the company. As none of this technology is available to me, I start to write – with a pen, on paper! I am making use of some of the things my imposter mum brought round at Easter which provide some of my work background. The rest I will have to make up. I have decided I will tell the "truth" about my accident and memory loss, which will at least be consistent with what everyone else thinks here.

That done, I make my way to where I saw the job advertised. It takes me about three-quarters of an hour as I wander along slowly looking in shop windows. I am still trying to keep my eyes open for some suitable clothes that appeal to me, but again I draw a blank.

The trade union office appears to be a hive of activity as I open the door. There is a receptionist immediately by the entrance, so I ask her if I might speak to someone about the secretarial vacancy they have advertised. I am asked to wait while she finds someone who can help me.

After about ten minutes a young woman appears, looking rather flustered. 'I'm sorry to keep you waiting but we are rather short-staffed today of all days,' she said. 'We have our annual conference in less than a week's time and there's a lot to get sorted yet.'

Her name is Iris and we spend the next ten minutes exchanging information about the requirements of the job and about my background and relevant experience. Of course, I cannot tell her how my real life revolves around having excellent keyboard skills for all the technology we take for granted, so she is no doubt rather wary of a soon-to-be unemployed English teacher with no apparent transferable skills. She does not seem concerned about my amnesia once I assure her that it only affects my past and that I have a good recall of everyday events and life in general since my accident.

We agree that I will come back tomorrow once a colleague can set up a typing test for me. I am also given an application form to complete and to bring back with me. I'm under the impression that they have no other candidates.

On my walk back to the flat I reflect on Iris, the office in general and the nature of the work described to me. I conclude that it could be quite a pleasant place to work, if they recruit me. The pay is considerably less than a teacher's pay but then that's not surprising as it does not require the same level of qualifications and skills.

When I get in, there is only Kate to talk to but she seems to think I am rushing in to a new job a bit too quickly. We talk about all kinds of things, including her girlfriend Anne. I'm amazed that she has not been invited to the flat yet even though they have been a couple for nearly a year and I suggest she should bring her round for a meal one weekend soon.

I spent the next half hour with Tom on my lap. He's a sweet cat but I really wish I could be with his namesake, my husband!

Finally, I sit at the dining table to complete the application form for tomorrow, making good use of the preparation I did earlier today.

Sue is cooking tonight. She announces that we are having convenience food as she is in a hurry. I'm intrigued to know what will be on offer. Coming from a world where freeze-dried, frozen and vacuum-packed ready meals are the norm I am wondering if I have been missing out on some delicacy.

Cooking sounds and smells are coming from the kitchen and in fact there has been considerable activity for almost an hour, so I'm wondering just how convenient this meal really is.

It turns out to be delicious. We have freshly peeled potatoes, carrots (which really taste like carrots, not the insipid soft things we get in my own time) and a Fray Bentos steak and kidney pie. The pie has puff pastry and came out of a tin which explains what Sue meant by convenience food. For afters we had tinned peaches and cream. The latter is actually Carnation evaporated milk out of a tin which is something I'm not familiar with but it tasted fine.

On Tuesday, as I head off to my interview and typing test, it occurs to me that I could bump into some of my pupils if I am passing by the school at the beginning or end of the day. Whilst that really should not matter, I do still have to let Mrs Staples know my decision so that she can formally accept my resignation. I make a mental note to telephone her when I get back. Oh, how much easier it is in my own time when a courteous email or even a text will suffice, rather than having to endure using that clumsy pay phone and leaving messages that do not get passed on.

In no time at all I arrive at the trade union office. The receptionist seems to recognise me today and is prepared for me. She takes me to an empty room and explains that in my own time (by that she means when I am ready!) I am to copy type the letter that is sitting next to a large manual typewriter. I have only ever seen pictures of this sort of monstrosity previously and somehow, I had expected a machine with at least some automation. Next to the typewriter was a pot of correcting fluid, which suggested that they thought I would make mistakes. I'll show them!

It did not take me long to complete the task, without mistakes I hasten to add, and when I had finished, I went back to the receptionist to see what was next. I was told to go back to the small room and she would send in the interview panel.

That sounded ominous but in fact it was only two people, Iris who I met yesterday and a man called Andrew. What followed seemed more like a conversation between friends than a formal interview. Iris complimented me on my typing and Andrew gave me a little more background on what the organisation did on a day to day basis. They finished by asking if I had any questions. I asked, very carefully, what equipment I would be expected to use and how many people worked here. Iris said there were two other typists, the receptionist and six trade union officials. One of the typists was just trying out an IBM golf-ball typewriter, which seemed to be the latest in high-tech as far as they were concerned. There was also a Gestetner machine for printing. I did not know what that was but I thought it would be unwise to show my total ignorance during the interview.

Suddenly the interview was over, there were handshakes and Iris asked me when I could start. I got the job! They did not need me to begin until their conference was over. They suggested that the Tuesday after the Bank Holiday would be an ideal time to start. I was happy with that. It gives me a couple of weeks, including my birthday when I suppose I should see my imposter parents, to get myself ready for this next adventure. That's if I have not managed to return to my own time by then.

14. Time Out in London

'Oh well done Jane,' said Sue, the minute she heard the news. 'I'm sure you will feel more at home in that office instead of the classroom.' Little did she know how much I was longing to be in my real home, in my own time. In the meantime (what a funny phrase that is, under the circumstances!) this job will have to do.

Angie's reaction was similar, 'Great news. What are you going to do between now and the beginning of May?'

I am beginning to think that Angie has been taking lessons from my imposter mum because before I could draw breath to answer the question, she offered a suggestion. 'I know! I will take a few days of my leave and we can go out, do some sightseeing and shopping!'

I accepted gracefully because once Angie gets an idea it is impossible to shift her thinking and, in any case, it will be good for us both to take some time out.

As it transpired, I had no idea how much fun it would be to see the sights of London in this era. In my real life, we don't often go far beyond Wimbledon even though we live in one of the most amazing capital cities in the world. For one thing, the options are limited unless you have plenty of money and in any case with two small boys, we can only take them out during the school holidays when everywhere is so busy and expensive. We keep hoping that once the boys are older, we can show them places of historical interest and take them to art galleries etc. Experiencing other places via Google Earth Virtual Reality is interesting but not really the same as being there. So, a 1970 "girls" outing or two with Angie should be fun.

Our first trip was on Sunday when we went to Portobello Road market. As well as the fruit and vegetable stalls, which in themselves were full of amazing produce from all over the world which I rarely see in my own time, there were dozens of sellers offering dresses, skirts, coats, jewellery and knick-knacks. The atmosphere was very relaxed and other shoppers seemed to know each other as I kept hearing them say to each other 'Peace and Love, man'.

I noticed that there was a powerful aroma of joss sticks everywhere. Angie told me they were used widely to mask the smell of marijuana. I don't know whether it was working but I was aware of quite a heady scent! In any case, we both relaxed and I decided I had better try to blend in by buying the kind of clothes people in this time were wearing.

I bought a long summer skirt which was tiered and made of a really pretty pink flowery material. Angie helped me to find a blouse that would go with it well and suggested that I could wear it with a black velvet choker. That evening I modelled my purchases for Sue and Kate and both of them approved!

We spent another day visiting London Zoo, which is close to Regent's Park. It was relaxing just wandering around looking at the animals. I haven't been to a zoo for years and it occurred to me it would be great to take Logan and Theo, if I ever get home to do so. The zoo was a pleasant surprise as all the animals appeared to have enough space and lived in well-designed environments so that it did not seem that they were trapped in cages. I would have liked to see more effort being made to support threatened species by captive breeding and returning them to the wild, as we do in my time.

Angie's leave was limited, so some days I went out on my own. I took the bus to Putney then the tube to Westminster, walked over the bridge and checked the time on my watch by Big Ben. Walking on the Embankment beside the Thames, this part of London looks quite strange and empty because many of the twenty-first century buildings that I am familiar with have not yet been built!

What I could not get used to was the number of people smoking, especially in the underground. I have got better at dealing with it since my first outing to the pub in Wimbledon but it is still a surprise and can be uncomfortable in an enclosed space. On the other hand, I found that complete strangers would strike up a conversation on public transport and were really friendly. Mostly, the talk was just about the weather but it made me feel less lonely.

In my own time no one speaks to anyone else because they all have their eyes glued to their tablets and phones. There is also an over-riding fear that if someone of the opposite gender is too friendly, they could be accused of sexual harassment. It's sad really that we seem to have lost the desire and the ability to communicate naturally with other people.

The other thing I noticed was that, in my own time, I would be taking photos of all the sights on my phone. Here, I just enjoyed looking and committing observations to memory.

My last day out with Angie involved even more walking. We walked to Southfields and took the District line to High Street Kensington. Our walking tour included Chelsea, Kensington Market, Carnaby Street and the Kings Road. I have no idea how we got around to all those places but Angie was a good guide and I just trotted along beside her while we chatted. I loved Kensington and actually bought some more clothes; Angie took her role as adviser seriously and encouraged me to buy a couple of summer dresses, a pair of denim jeans, two tee-shirts and a pullover. I was hoping she would not steer me towards Marks & Spencer which she said was really expensive and specialised in underwear and clothes for older people, although she made good use of her insider knowledge to compare the clothes and their prices.

On the days I did not go out with Angie, I amused myself at home. I found in a drawer an old cameo brooch which I imagine belonged to an elderly relative of the other Jane. I had already bought some black velvet ribbon so I made the choker Angie had suggested, adorned with the cameo. It looked good.

I also had another visit to the library but again I drew a blank in terms of discovering if there were other examples of people finding themselves in the wrong time. One of the librarians asked if she could help but I thought it would be unwise to say what I was looking for. She encouraged me to join the library so that I could borrow a book to read. It was kind, but in truth I just wanted my e-reader so that I could download everything.

One day I came across a church jumble sale and went inside to discover that all sorts of nice things like home-made cakes, books and clothes were being sold to raise money for the church building. I found a gorgeous navy-blue dress patterned with pink cherry blossom and large red cherries. I held it up to myself and it looked as if it would fit. They only charged two shillings and six pence, which I learned is "half a crown". When I got back to the flat, I tried it on and it is perfect! In my own time we have charity shops that sell second hand clothes but I doubt I'd get a quality bargain like this.

I took advantage of the spare time to have my hair cut, returning it to something like my usual neat bob and removing all the curly bits that were still slightly in evidence. I was rather afraid that I would accidentally come across the hairdresser who did the original afro perm. On the other hand, I don't really know how that happened since it wasn't me but the Jane who normally lives here. Oh, I don't know. I get more and more confused about what has happened to me.

By the end of my time off I received a letter from the Education Authority confirming that my resignation had been accepted and explaining about my pension. I cried for a bit but tried hard not to think about the implications if I was still here by the time I got to pension age.

I also had a letter from my new employer with a contract and terms and conditions, as well as a form to return with my bank details so that my pay could go directly into my account. It's strange that everything goes by post and takes several days to arrive.

On May 2nd my flatmates treated me to a special tea as it was my birthday and we all went out to the cinema. We saw "The Italian Job" with Michael Caine, Noel Coward and Benny Hill. It was a light-hearted comedy and I enjoyed it as much as I could, under the circumstances.

Another evening, Kate asked everyone if we could help her prepare for the Nursery Open Day. This involved me cutting ducks – the sort children play with in the bath – from yellow cardboard. Angie was roped in to write in big letters A is for Apple, B is for Ball etc as she has really neat handwriting. Sue had to paint fairies as she is really artistic. We had a lot of fun, especially as Angie found a bottle of Cinzano that she had won in a raffle so by the end of the evening we were all quite tipsy.

It's at times like these I can almost believe that this is my real life and I try to pretend that I don't really come from the twenty-first century. The trouble is, I really have not got used to being alone again and my heart aches for Tom and the boys. I try not to think about the prospect of never seeing Tom again, never going to sleep in his arms, never enjoying our discussions over the dinner table. He is my perfect partner and I have been very fortunate to spend the last eleven years with him.

Of course, we have proved everyone wrong who said it would never last. I suppose high-tailing it off to Gretna Green with a man they barely knew must have been worrying for my grandparents. At the time it seemed like the most romantic thing in the world and in any case, it avoided all the fuss of a big wedding. We had known each other for almost two years, it was just that they were not aware of that.

It was my Dad/Grandad's fault, sort-of. He works in advertising in a job which is linked to film and television. Because of this, there are always famous people in our house and most weekends they have parties for the movers and shakers of the time. Growing up in this environment held little appeal for me although a few of the contacts have been very useful subsequently in my recruitment job.

I became used to adult conversation and I learned to sit quietly while MPs, bankers, men – and often women – who were CEOs of big businesses all chatted over our dining table.

So, Tom and I met (this is not a cliché) in the kitchen at one of their parties. I was sixteen and he was a couple of months older. He had been dragged along by his dad because he was under the impression that he couldn't trust Tom to behave sensibly in the house alone. Of course, it wasn't true, but I could completely sympathise with the embarrassment he felt having to tag along with his dad when he would have preferred to be out with his mates. Tom's dad is an MP and had something important to discuss with my grandad.

Now most of my schoolfriends at the time had boyfriends that they had either met at school or were friends of friends they connected with through social media. I just had not really bothered about boys other than seeing them as "just mates" as my life was complicated enough as it was. Tom did not have a girlfriend and so we sort of got talking and suddenly the evening flew by and we had both enjoyed talking to each other. I told Tom what had happened to my birth parents and he was sweetly thoughtful about not asking me distressing questions.

My grandparents were very protective of me, so I decided it would be best to keep my friendship with Tom private. It was easy to tell them I was meeting my friends Gill or Andrea to go shopping or to check homework. After a while, it just became a habit. Tom's dad was aware of our growing relationship and curiously it never occurred to me that he would tell anyone. As it happened, he didn't.

Once the end of school life beckoned, I was terrified that I would have to go away to University and would only be able to see Tom during the holidays. Tom was already making a name for himself in the IT world and he had assumed we would eventually get a flat together.

One dreadful day, we had a massive argument about the future. Tom was happy to jog along as we were and it had not crossed his mind that I might be "banished/ sent away" as I described it, perhaps a bit overdramatically. After we had kissed and made up, he asked what I wanted to do. Gretna Green seemed like a simple solution and so that was what we did the very next weekend. I didn't even have a special dress or a bridesmaid. I got what I wanted though, the man of my dreams as my very own husband.

When we got back, the parents were incandescent with rage! They blamed me, Tom, Tom's dad, in fact everyone they could think of. Eventually, everyone got over it and wished us all the happiness in the world, even if it wasn't going to last. That was 2018 and we are still together. Well, we were, until this dreadful thing happened to me.

Mind you, whilst all this being in the wrong century is a disaster for me, I think I was mistaken about the world being a gentler place right now. I suppose the "Peace and Love" and "sex, drugs and rock & roll" culture that I find myself thrown into has blinded me to the brutality taking place elsewhere. I pick some of these things up on the radio. For example, it came to light last year that some American soldiers had committed a massacre at My Lai which raised very many questions about the way the Vietnam war was being conducted or even whether it was the right thing for America to be involved in.

Recently, thousands of people of all ages have been demonstrating in America against President Nixon with much of the anger being evident in University campuses across the country. Only yesterday there was the appalling news at Kent State University that the Ohio National Guard had opened fire at a student demonstration and four students had been shot dead.

I haven't discussed this with my flatmates yet but I'm sure they will be horrified that such a thing could happen.

15. New Job

My first morning in the new job is both exciting and nerve-wracking. To begin with, Iris took me round each office and introduced me to everyone. I hope I can remember all their names as no-one seems to have any difficulty with mine.

The receptionist is Joan; she's been here for many years, knows everyone and is the fount of all knowledge I'm told. She is, how do I put this politely? quite a large lady. I haven't worked out yet if she is friendly; she seems a bit of an ogre.

Inside the main office, where my desk is, there are the two other secretaries Florence and Sylvia. They both seem very pleasant and, I would guess they are both much older than me, perhaps in their fifties. I assumed this from the sort of clothes they are wearing apart from the obvious grey hair and wrinkles! I was wearing a miniskirt today and from their expressions I could guess they think it's a bit trendy for the office. Clearly, they are keen to get to know everything about me, which is out of the question but hopefully I can tell them enough to satisfy their curiosity. I shall, of course, counter their questions with some of my own which should make it interesting!

The trade union officials, including Andrew who I met at my interview, sit in the back office. They were not all in the office today and I believe they are mostly out and about working with trade union members around the country. I was introduced to a couple of them and told the names of the rest (there are six altogether) and promptly forgot them. I wonder if there really is something to this amnesia?

Across the corridor from the reception area is the stock cupboard which is really a small room which houses the Gestetner machine, shelves of pre-printed letterhead paper, paper and envelopes of all sizes and a selection of pens, paperclips and files.

Next door is the kitchen which is self-explanatory although I did ask Iris why there were so many cups and saucers on the worktop. She explained that when meetings and courses were held on site, in the two large conference rooms upstairs, someone has to make the visitors' coffee. From the knowing look she gave me I suspect that someone will be me.

The toilets are upstairs, and I did remark that this seems a bit inconvenient, but I don't think Iris appreciated my feeble attempt at a joke. At least I shall keep fit what with transporting coffees and tidying the conference rooms after an event.

Sylvia and Florence were only too happy to tell me how things work here. For instance, no one has their own secretary and any typing that is required is placed in a tray by the senior staff. We have to take whatever is on the top, type it and leave it in another tray for the person to collect it.

I try hard not to smile visibly because in my real world no one has a secretary because everyone types things directly into their tablet or laptop. We use voice recognition software quite a lot too. Here, if the work involves making phone calls to organise or book something then the trade union official will write down the task and leave it in the tray also. I'm inclined to think this is all a massive job creation scheme until I see the antiquated typewriter I am expected to use. I thought the one they gave me for my typing test at the interview was just to assess my ability but I seem to have inherited the oldest piece of kit in the building.

Anyway, all this seems to take up quite a lot of the morning, so it is almost time for elevenses they tell me. I don't know whether the pace of work is generally this relaxed or if it is just because it is the day after a Bank Holiday. Of course, the big annual conference is out of the way too so maybe everyone is getting over that. Sylvia asks me how I like my coffee and I tell her quite strong and not too much milk.

'Did you bring a mug?' she enquires. I mentally add that to my "to-do list" and so we use a spare one with a Trade Union logo on it.

As the in-tray seems to have grown considerably by the time we get back from the kitchen with our hot mugs of coffee, I take the first piece and prepare to type. Florence is watching me closely and before I can begin, she reminds me that I will need what she calls 'a top sheet, a carbon and a flimsy'. These have to be put together in the correct order, making sure that they are level and then fed into the typewriter around the roller. I discover that this is how copies for the file are produced, which now I come to think about it, is obvious. If you do not have a key to press for multiple copies and you cannot store a copy electronically, then this rather messy approach is essential. I smile my thanks and hope I do not appear too ignorant of the ways of the office.

Fortunately, I reprieve myself by typing a whole letter without making any mistakes, which was especially pleasing after Sylvia had brought over to my desk a small bottle of Tippex correcting fluid.

Before long, it is lunch break and both ladies bring out their Tupperware boxes containing a sandwich (Sylvia) and a salad (Florence). I had not thought about this in advance so when asked, I said I would pop out for something. Florence gave a little purse of the lips to indicate she thought I was rather profligate with my money if I was going to buy something rather than prepare it at home. I decided not to let this reaction trouble me. By going out to buy a sandwich at least that would reduce the amount of time I would be closely interrogated on my life and secretarial experience!

As I went out, Joan asked me where I was going for lunch. I said I didn't know yet and she mentioned that when the Theatre was open for a matinee, they do a good line in snacks and sandwiches. It was not open today but it was kind of Joan to let me know for the future. Here I am thinking about how I will be working here in the future, when all I want to do is go back to my own time.

A brisk walk along the High Street brought me to the small Sainsbury's supermarket where I bought a ready-made cheese sandwich and a packet of crisps. I found a seat near to the railway station and ate my lunch watching the world go by. The crisp packet contained a small blue bag of salt which had to be untwisted and shaken into the bag to coat the crisps. I enjoyed this short break from my first day at the new job.

By the time I got back, having made sure I did not overrun the allotted three-quarters of an hour lunch break, both Florence and Sylvia were hard at it, clattering away on their typewriters.

Florence was preparing a letter that would have multiple copies so she very kindly took me through the process for using the large printing machine. I'm not sure I have ever heard of Gestetner but it was helpful to see how to use it, even though it was a cumbersome and potentially messy business. It made me realise how much I take for granted my home printer and the office photocopier in my own time.

By afternoon tea-break my two colleagues were desperate to find out more about me so I put them out of their misery by giving them my carefully constructed story about getting run over by a bus, in a coma in hospital, fully recovered now apart from a "patch of amnesia" covering the last ten years or so. I explained that although I did return to teaching briefly, it was too challenging for me and I realised that I needed a change of direction. I pre-empted any questions about husbands or boyfriends by explaining that I was very happy sharing a flat with three friends and had no serious relationship. That kept them fully entertained during the tea-break and when Andrew came in to collect some letters he had left for us, the conversation ground to a rapid halt.

In this way, my first week has passed quite pleasantly and I feel I am settling in well.

Thursday May 14th
All sorts of things have been happening at work this week. First, Florence got her new typewriter which is an IBM golfball. Basically, it has a number of round metal balls with the alphabet on, which click into place and provide the typist with different typefaces. It is partly

electronic which means one doesn't have to bang so hard on the keys like the old manual things that Sylvia and I have to use. She is loving it and I'm sure it has increased the office productivity considerably.

I seem to be getting on well with the senior people here. I was in the back office and Paul involved me in a discussion about employment contracts - not for here but in some of the companies where they have members. I have a feeling he knows I have quite a bit of background in this which didn't come from being a teacher! Andrew also makes a point of asking my opinion on things, as well as asking me to call him Andy now.

Friday May 15th
Florence and Sylvia are determined to treat me as the office junior and I get all the "gofer" tasks. That includes watering the pot plants, going out to buy a jar of coffee and tidying the room upstairs after a meeting. I suppose I am the most junior (although I prefer to see it as being younger than all the others) so I shall have to put up with it for now. In any case, they are only basing their actions on the modest autobiography, I have created for them.

I still have difficulty remembering that we have no photocopier, no instant messaging and no mobile phones. On a daily basis, I have to stop myself saying 'Oh, just Google it!' or 'But you can get that on Amazon!'. I long to be back in my own time, not for those things, but to be with my family. I do wish I could find how to get back.

16. Making Friends

'Bye, Jane. Have a good weekend,' says Sylvia as she hurries out of the office door. Florence has already left as, for some bizarre reason, we are supposed to work until four-thirty on a Friday instead of leaving at 5:30 each day. I am just finishing off a short memo. Once that is done, I will head off too, not that I have anything interesting to do.

Andy puts his head round the door. 'Oh, I didn't realise that was the time. Sorry Jane, is there any chance you could do this letter for me as I need to get it in the post?' I smile as of course I'm happy to do it.

'I need fifty copies; do you know how to use the Gestetner?' he asked. 'Sure, no problem. Florence showed me what to do last week.'

Andy returns to his office and I hear his soft voice on the phone. I suppose he's calling his wife to tell her he will be a bit late.

Fixing the waxy stencil onto my antiquated typewriter is tricky but I type the brief letter quite quickly, check it for spelling mistakes (although I do miss the automatic spell-checker from my own time), attach the stencil to the Gestetner drum, check the ink level and begin to turn the handle. It hasn't taken me long to run off the copies and as I am really pleased with myself for managing the job without asking questions, I go straight into Andy's office with the finished product.

'Here we are, Andy,' I declare with a flourish. 'Oh. Erm. You didn't bring it in for me to sign the stencil before you ran off the copies, Jane!'

I am so embarrassed. How stupid of me not to think this through before letting my over-enthusiasm for proving my worth take over.

'I'm really sorry, Andy. I didn't realise,' I say.
'Never mind, I will just have to sign them all individually now,' he said with a grin. 'You can start on addressing the envelopes and then we will set up a production line with a sign, fold, label, seal and stamp system. It won't take us long.'

It is good of him not to complain as he signs fifty letters individually and in fact it is quite pleasant sitting alongside him. It is good to be working with someone, as opposed to the silent concentration which pervades the typing office. We joke with each other as we work and it does not feel like a chore in any way.

'Well done. That was verging on being enjoyable,' said Andy, as the last stamp was put on the envelope. 'Now as it is gone six and I have cruelly kept you back at work, I think I should take you out for a drink and something to eat.'

I'm a bit taken aback at this and unsure how to react. 'Oh, there's no need, Andy. My flatmates will have held back my meal so I will just head for home now,' I blushed. 'I was happy to help out and sorry again about making you sign fifty letters!'

I have reflected on this over the weekend and concluded that **IF** Andy is single, then there would be no harm in accepting a friendly invitation like this. I am less happy about him taking me out if he is married, of course. Although I cannot really claim the moral high ground here. I also experienced a twinge of conscience that I could even consider going out with a colleague for a social evening when I am so far away in time from my family. Surely, I shouldn't be enjoying myself?

The weekend has flown by and before I notice it, it's Monday again and I'm actually looking forward to work. I wish I was in my own time with my family but until I can work out how to get home, I am trying to make the most of the new experiences that come my way.

Following the lead of Florence and Sylvia, I have started to take lunch to work rather than buying a sandwich on the way in, although I often find I am eating it in the back office with Paul, Andy, Brian, Iris or George. I haven't met Chris yet as she has been working up in Scotland.

They are an amusing crowd and I always seem to learn something interesting. I have a feeling Florence and Sylvia disapprove because they have a very rigid view of office hierarchy, but I'm taking no notice of them. Joan doesn't get involved in these inter-office issues as she usually eats her lunch at the reception desk. I suppose that's so she can direct visitors as well as being on hand to answer the switchboard. She's actually very kind and thoughtful and not the ogre I first imagined.

We do discuss the news and occasionally politics but the things that intrigue me most are the day-to-day issues that are so different to my real life. For example, in my own time we have lots of different fast-food outlets providing snacks and meals which have originated in many countries around the world. I don't think they bear much resemblance to authentic Chinese, Thai, Greek etc meals but they are handy when one is in a hurry. The only one that I am aware of round here is the Wimpey Bar, which is on Station Bridge. I have been in there a couple of times and it is quite pleasant, especially as the burgers are made from real meat.

Paul was telling us this lunchtime that women are not allowed inside the Wimpey Bar after midnight, unless they are accompanied by a man. I couldn't believe this but the reason for the ban assumes that if they are alone, they must be prostitutes! I said that it was unlikely there would be many women affected by the ban because who wants to eat burgers after midnight? Everyone laughed. I think they enjoy my company as I do theirs.

After lunchtime on Friday and just as I was getting down to a job for Iris which involved making a lot of phone calls to set up a meeting, Andy put his head round the office door and asked quietly if he could have a word with me. He gestured to the corridor so that we could speak privately.

'I was wondering if you would like to try that new Italian restaurant that opened recently in the town?' Before I had a chance to say anything he followed up with, 'we could have lunch there tomorrow, then you won't be risking eating late or spoiling a meal your flatmates have prepared for you!'

'Thank you. That sounds like a good idea, Andy,' and rapidly thinking on my feet I said, 'but wouldn't you rather be spending the Bank Holiday weekend with your family?' For an off-the-cuff reaction I thought I did rather well.

'No, I have no family except my parents who live up North and I would much rather have lunch with you,' he replied.

Friday May 22nd
So here I am feeling a mixture of trepidation and excitement, wondering what to wear and what the restaurant will be like tomorrow. I'm not sure if this is a date but I don't think it can do any harm to have lunch with a relatively new friend while I am trying to sort my life out.

17. The Date

How strange to be going out on a sort-of date. Lunch with Andy is, after all, just eating out with a colleague as a variation on eating my sandwich in his office along with a number of other colleagues. I am trying to convince myself that this is nothing to get excited about but, after being married to Tom for nine years and being totally faithful to him even before that, it does seem odd to be dining out at a restaurant with another man.

Of course, Kate, Sue and Angie are intrigued and offer much encouragement. I had not actually mentioned Andy before, other than just describing the people I work with in a very cursory way. As far as I can tell, they think the Jane they know has been single for far too long.

'You remember that Friday when I had to work late? Well, it's just a thank you for that. Nothing else.'

I'm not sure who I was trying to convince but I did get caught up in their excitement for me, using the evening to try on various outfits in order to get their seal of approval. Angie insisted on lending me a clutch purse which would match the skirt and top we bought on the Portobello Road.

'Where is he taking you, then?' asked Sue.

'I'm not sure. I think it is a new Italian restaurant in town.'

'Oh. Wow,' said Angie. 'You mean San Lorenzo!'

Suddenly my world jolted. It must be the same place that Tom and I have been to when we can afford it and can book a babysitter. I had no idea it had been around since the 1970s. Would anyone recognise me? I did a quick calculation and realised there was no chance of that unless the waiters were truly in their dotage. It did make me feel uncomfortable though.

By the time Saturday morning arrived I was really feeling jittery. What if Andy questions me about my life and background? What if he expects me to know about something from the 60's like a TV programme or a famous person? What if we both feel embarrassed because it isn't really anything to do with work and we might not know what to talk about? Even the warm, scented bath that Angie ran for me failed to soothe my jangling nerves.

Then, there was a tap at the door and he was there! We both smile at each other. He looks good in his non-work clothes; more relaxed and younger. I don't know how old he is but that's what this lunch is about – an opportunity to get to know each other as friends.

'I didn't bring the car Jane, as it's not far to walk and the sun is shining.'

We headed off slowly up Viney Hill, along Lake Road and past Ricards Lodge School, where I tried hard not to think about bailing out of my teaching commitments, then a short stretch along Woodside and there we were at San Lorenzo. I'm not sure what we talked about but I felt extremely relaxed and comfortable.

The restaurant looks familiar, but different. I must have walked past the place repeatedly since I arrived in this time but I just had not recognised it before. At the door, Andy stood to one side so that I could go in first. These "old-fashioned courtesies" are no longer practised in the twenty-first century and I found it quite charming.

'I have a table for two booked for one o'clock in the name of Wood'
'Welcome Mr Wood and guest. Please come in and Mauro will show you to your table'.

We spent a few minutes in silence studying the menu. Bear in mind that in my real life I am quite familiar with Italian food but this restaurant was an innovation for a 1970's London suburb. I thought it best to appear unfamiliar with the dishes so I asked Andy if he had any suggestions. Good move, Jane!

We both chose a seafood starter and a pasta dish for our main course. Andy asked the waiter what wine would be suitable to go with our meal and he advised a crisp white wine. I reminded myself again that in this time, it was probable that eating out at a restaurant with food from another country was not an everyday occurrence and wine was very much a luxury.

Once the practical arrangements were in place Andy directed his deep brown eyes to me. 'You intrigue me Jane,' he said softly. 'You are on the surface very straightforward; a hard-working secretary sharing a flat with girlfriends, attractive and sensible with a delightful sense of humour.' I smiled at the compliments although I could sense there was a 'but' coming.

'The Jane I would like to get to know has hidden depths, life experiences that I can only partially guess at and, I imagine, aspirations she hasn't even considered yet.'

Well you could certainly say that! As I felt this observation was rapidly treading on dangerous ground and, as our first course was being delivered discreetly to our table, I turned the conversation back to Andy.

'I think I could say some similar things about you, Andy! I would like to know a bit about where you were born, what you enjoyed as a child and how come you are working for a trade union? My past is not a secret but some of it is hidden because of the amnesia I suffered after the accident.'

Andy seemed to accept this and happily chatted about his family and upbringing in North Yorkshire. His choice of career, as so often is the case as I know from my real job, came about by accident. His schoolfriend Joseph had started work a couple of years before Andy and when his employer made some organisational changes that would have a considerable impact on his friend's work life and pay, he sought advice from his trade union. Andy was impressed by the help Joseph received which resulted in what I would call a "win-win" for the friend and his company. Then, after university Andy took up a work placement with a trade union which confirmed his thoughts and he concluded it would be a worthwhile path to follow.

By this stage our seafood starter, which was delicious, was already eaten and the plates cleared.

'Cheers Jane and thank you for agreeing to join me for lunch.' We clinked glasses and I realised the wine was going to my head straight away.

'So, what about you? It's your turn,' he grinned.

'There's nothing really mysterious about me, Andy. I am quite a private person but always happy to share things with people I like and respect.'

He smiled at the veiled compliment before I continued by saying a little about my imposter parents and some history that I have gleaned from the things mum brought me once I got out of hospital. 'As for career choice, well it wasn't really my idea but I went into teaching to please my parents. To be honest, the accident – although it and the amnesia have been unpleasant – did me a favour and I don't regret for a moment leaving teaching. I'm enjoying my secretarial job and happy to learn from it, for now.'

Andy nodded thoughtfully. I assume my responses were acceptable and to be honest they were not far from the truth, apart from omitting to mention that I was born in a different era. Being married, with children, was of course not part of this conversation either.

By the time our main courses arrived, which looked lovely and were really tasty, we were well into discussing music, hobbies and interests in general.
I had forgotten how enjoyable it can be to eat a leisurely meal with a friend. Andy is good company and it was not only the wine that made me feel so relaxed.

When Mauro came over with the dessert trolley for us, we agreed that we were both too full to eat any more but decided that it would be worth coming back to this restaurant another time as there were so many temptations on the menu. The time had just flown by and it was almost four o'clock when we finished our espresso coffees.

I wasn't sure of dating etiquette having not done it for so long, not that this was really a date.

'That was a great meal, thank you Andy. Can we "go dutch"?'
'No. Certainly not. It was my invitation and I have really enjoyed myself too.'

He leant forward and gently lifted the hair out of my eyes. I think my accident scar which it was covering, has almost disappeared. 'I hope we can continue to see each other, not just at work,' he said. I smiled back but was unsure how to respond further.

Andy paid the bill with crisp paper notes, leaving a tip for our waiter and again I realised how different everything is in my own time where cashless payment is the norm.

Once outside the restaurant, it was turning a little cold and naturally Andy put his arm round me to keep the wind at bay. We ambled back to Viney Hill talking all the way.

'Would you like to come in to meet my flatmates?'

'Not this time thank you Jane, as I have a few things to do before the shops close. I would like to spend some time with you again. Are you free at all this Bank Holiday weekend?'

'I've got nothing planned for Monday.'

'How about a walk round Cannizaro Park?'

'Oh, that would be good. I've never been there, even though it is on the doorstep.'

'Right. I'll come round for you about eleven-thirty. We can have a lunchtime drink in the Hand-in-Hand pub and afternoon tea in the tearooms. Bring a waterproof just in case the weather turns and wear sturdy footwear. Would that be OK?'

My grin must have been all the response Andy needed and with that he planted a kiss on my cheek and strode off towards the town.

18. Just Good Friends?

I had such a good time today. Cannizaro Park was quite lively with couples and families out to enjoy the Bank Holiday. Other people it seems, according to Andy, were happy to sit in their cars amongst the petrol and diesel fumes in order to head for the seaside.

I don't really know how to deal with my friendship with Andy. I enjoy his company immensely yet I feel I am being utterly disloyal to Tom. I feel guilty for enjoying my outing with this new friend. In some ways, finding myself in another time and losing my husband and children is like a bereavement. I switch between feeling angry that this has happened totally outside my control, monumentally sad to have lost the family I love and relieved that I am managing in my new life without anyone suspecting that I am not the Jane they know. I worry a lot about whether Tom and the boys are managing without me maybe even thinking I have disappeared or whether there is another version of me with them.

Andy is a good man but of course I'm not comfortable about him not knowing who I really am. Every time I think about it, I am in turmoil. I am, after all, a wife and mother. I've got the stretch marks to prove it! Although when I checked my stomach the other day, those stretch marks were only visible with the eye of faith.

I am genuinely enjoying some aspects of living in 1970 as it is almost like being on an adventure holiday. That is, apart from the aspects I don't like. On the other hand, there is an unfortunately a long list of moans.

The lack of any sensible system for communicating anything mildly complex means that we have to write it down and post it, waiting for a response by mail a week later.

Using the telephone is a tedious business; each call requires a string of numbers to be physically dialled and if the person is not in, we have to do it again another time and keep on until they are available. It also has to be done wherever the phone is located in your house or office. It had never occurred to me how flexible a mobile phone is, until I didn't have one anymore!

In my own time no one uses a fixed landline telephone anymore. Trying to co-ordinate six people who will be coming to a meeting, which was what I was doing at work last week, is a nightmare here. If only I could have sent a one-line email it could have been sorted in minutes.

Similarly, the effort involved in obtaining information is beyond belief! If I ever get back to my own time, I will never again say in such a blasé manner "I'll check the website". The lack of the internet is incalculable. No matter whether I want to know how to get somewhere, or to find out about another country and its customs and history, or look up a book, a play, a piece of art or sculpture in my own time it is at my fingertips. I may have been guilty of moaning about electronic overload but honestly, I miss it so much here.

Not to mention the tedium of shopping! Of course, it had not occurred to me to begin with, that in 1970 shopping involves going to lots of places to search for things and coming away without buying. In my own time if you can think of it, you can probably buy it – all without leaving the comfort of your chair. It will arrive the next day by drone or in a van. In a nutshell, lack of technology means everything has to be done by hand, slowly. It drives me mad!

I am finding attitudes difficult to adjust to here, as well. People are dreadfully racist, sexist and ageist and ignorant of difference in the true sense of the word. I have tried to do a little discreet study in the library into attitudes towards homosexuality and I discover that it is relatively recently (barely three years ago) that gay men were no longer imprisoned. Hard to believe, I know.

The law on homosexuality does not seem to relate to women and only addresses relationships between men over the age of 18, where both adults consent. While the law has changed, attitudes have not and I am truly embarrassed and mortified by the things some people say. No wonder Kate is very discreet about her special friendship with Anne.

Don't get me started on racism either. In spite of slavery being at an end, thankfully, the way some people of colour are treated is disgraceful. No one seems to challenge this insulting state of affairs and as prejudice is not against the law, people just get away with it.

In my own time, I was vaguely aware of the 1960s and the history of beatniks, hippies, travellers and people who chose to live a bohemian lifestyle. It is rather different to find oneself parachuted into this time. It is so much more than fashions, music and drug-taking and I am only just grasping the impact all that has on culture, beliefs and attitudes. Although that decade is over, the world is now changed as a result – at least, the part of the world I am having to inhabit.

Some other things are what I suppose are known as hygiene factors, although now I come to think about that phrase, it probably correctly refers to motivation at work. You see, if only I could have checked that on the internet, I would not have made that mistake. Anyway, I mean how dirty everywhere is. The streets are littered with cigarette ends, empty fag packets, chewing gum and dog poo. Honestly, it is filthy everywhere. Pets are allowed to walk the streets at will. I would not dream of allowing Dog to wander around defecating on pavements and in people's gardens. That's disgusting!

That thought has reminded me of Dog. I miss him too because he's one of the family. Having Tom cat here is a minor compensation, I suppose.

I promised myself that I would resolve how I feel about Andy, before going to bed. All I have done all evening is have a silent rant to myself about the difficulty of living in 1970. I don't know if I will ever get used to things here.

<u>Monday May 25th</u>
It is time I went to bed but I still have not tackled the big issues from today. Do I let my friendship with Andy continue? How can I get back to my own time?

My conclusions so far are that it is OK carry on seeing Andy (I cannot avoid him at work, anyway) because I may be here for a very long time if not forever. There is no problem about being just good friends surely.

I should be more creative about getting back. I remember hurrying to work that last morning so I am going to explore the road and pavement where everything seemed to change. That might sound silly but I cannot come up with anything better. Goodnight diary and thank you for letting me talk to you.

P.S. Tuesday morning – am I going mad, talking to a notebook?!

19. Change is Afoot

I am back at work for the last few days of May and it occurs to me that I have already been away from my real home for more than two months. So far, no one has noticed that I am not the Jane they knew, which is odd, although I am thankful not to have to deal with that. Equally, no one has questioned me on how long the amnesia is likely to last so I continue to use that as an excuse if my behaviour seems unexpected or if I say something inappropriate.

When not in the office, I am getting used to watching the television with my flatmates but I have to be honest, I don't share their tastes. They watch Coronation Street which is a series set in the North of England, based around a public house. I usually manage to avoid this one. Of the various comedies they watch, I have difficulty with the racism and other forms of prejudice expressed by the characters. Steptoe and Son is one of those. It's about a "rag and bone man" and his son. These are people who drive round the streets with a horse and cart collecting other people's rubbish for a living. Of course, we have recycling centres in my own time so it's all a bit unfamiliar to me. Steptoe and his son are horrible to each other and it is mostly based on lack of understanding between the generations. The ageism is meant to be funny. It isn't. It's not that I don't have a sense of humour, I just think poking fun at stereotypes is a bit unsophisticated.

We do all sit down together to watch Top of the Pops once a week; the selection of music playing on this programme depends on the popularity of the band or musician and their success in the sales charts. People can only buy music on vinyl disks here but I have a feeling that it makes better quality sound reproduction than in my own time; perhaps that's why it's called high fidelity.

By contrast, in the 21st century, music is streamed on line and made public on U-Tube and other applications. Some of the music they play on the radio here is great and my favourites at the moment are "All Right Now" by Free and "I'm a Man" by Jimi Hendrix. Kate plays the LP, which is short for Long Player, "Bridge Over Troubled Water" by Simon and Garfunkel incessantly while Angie is heavily into anything by The Beatles. She was heartbroken when they broke up recently, although the others both said it had been on the cards for ages.

The only TV programme I watch avidly is Dr Who. This is set in the future, although nothing in it resembles the future that I am familiar with. What is interesting is that the main character, the Doctor, is a time traveller. He uses a Police Box to travel in, which is not much use to me as most of these boxes have been removed here since the police stopped using them. The only police box I have seen in the twenty-first century is a tourist attraction. Apparently, they were used by the police here relatively recently in order to access a landline telephone to communicate with their base station. It's hilarious to think how slow and pedestrian everything is here without mobile phones. At least, it's amusing except when I am trying to get something done. I enjoy the Dr Who programme although I am not hopeful that it will show me how to get back to my own time.

'Jane, are you coming to watch the party-political broadcast?' calls Angie. I cannot really refuse as everyone seems very excited about the forthcoming General Election.

Sue bounces into the room with more enthusiasm than I am used to seeing her display normally. 'Mum is coming down to help me choose my dress,' she announces and immediately I realise this is something I should be aware of. I'm not sure what it is about so I smile and keep quiet.

'Have you had any ideas?' asks Angie.

'Not a clue. I expect Mum will be in full organising mode. Pete doesn't want it to be too formal though.'

She turns to me, 'Do you want to bring Andy, Jane?'

I look rather blankly back at her and I'm hesitating whether to say yes or no.

'Oh no. That's not something else you have forgotten, Jane? Surely you know that the wedding of the year is coming up on August 1st?' reacts Angie.

'Err. Well it may have slipped my mind. Sorry Sue,' I grinned. 'I'm not sure yet whether it would be appropriate to ask Andy but thank you anyway. Can I let you know?'

After the General Election programme, which was rather upstaged by Sue's wedding dress announcement, the national news came on. The newsreaders are very formal and careful not to influence opinion so there was nothing controversial other than some information about employment legislation which I really should have paid attention to as it could be useful for work. A brief item of international news showed thousands of protesters demonstrating in New York against the Vietnam War and from what I can gather there are equally numerous and vociferous pro-war demonstrations. I listened quietly to Angie and Sue discuss the issue but I try not to take a side. In my own time, we have current time reporting via social media which may be heavily biased but we do at least hear what actual people on the ground think.

While this was going on, Kate very quietly came into the room and sat next to me. At a convenient pause in the debate, she cleared her throat to announce: 'I just thought everyone would like to know that I may be moving.'

We all looked expectantly at her. 'My friend Anne has asked if I would like to move to her place.'

I sensed this could provoke an unwanted reaction so I leapt in immediately with 'Oh, Kate. That's lovely news! Are congratulations in order then?'

Angie and Sue both looked surprised but did not know what to say.

'It won't be for a couple of months, probably not until the end of August but I thought I should let you know so you can find someone to rent my room.'

'We haven't met Anne yet, why don't you ask her round for Sunday lunch?' suggested Sue and immediately the tension was dissipated.

The next day, in the office, I asked Andy if he would like to come over for Sunday lunch. I thought it would help Anne feel less of an outsider if she was not the only guest.

'Thank you, Jane. That would be lovely. Are you sure you will have room?'

'Could you bring two extra chairs, by any chance?'

'Oh, so I'm not the only honoured guest!'

'That's right. Kate has invited her partner Anne too.'

I don't think it was my imagination but I'm sure that Florence and Sylvia exchanged a "look". I was tempted to say something but, in the end, I kept quiet because they were already critical of my friendship with Andy. In their opinion, it was not appropriate for work colleagues to embark on a relationship. In fact, they both seem to have rather forceful views about all sorts of things. It's a pity they do not direct their attention to the many prejudices and injustices I see all around me. I can only hope that they would begin to see things differently if one of their offspring turned out to be gay.

On the night of June 19th, we four flatmates sat up late, glued to the television while the results of the General Election came in. We had not discussed how each of us voted but I'm pretty sure that we all voted Labour, although the area where we live is a Conservative stronghold. The conversation was mainly about returning the current Labour government. From the exit polls this looked to be a likely outcome so eventually each of us went to bed as we still had to go to work on Friday.

Imagine our surprise in the morning when we discovered from the radio that Edward Heath, the leader of the Conservative party had won and Harold Wilson the Prime Minister had conceded. I don't know what changes that will bring about but I imagine there will be an impact on us all.

Aside from the election, life continues as normal. Andy and I went to the cinema this Saturday. We saw Butch Cassidy and the Sundance Kid. I have a feeling I had heard of this film in my own time; it was good anyway, so it probably merits being a classic.

As ever, I enjoyed his company as much as the film. I suppose it's got nothing to do with the admiring glances that I get when out with him. He is one of those men with classically good looks. A sort of 1970's George Clooney. Whatever it is, I do notice other women looking at him. He's good fun to be with too. We have these games where we privately make up stories about people we see in the street. Nothing unkind. Just using our imagination. For example, there was a couple in the cinema sitting in front of us. It appeared that they had had a bad argument before they came out and they were barely speaking to each other. During most of the walk back to Viney Hill we were making up stories about what they had fallen out over and what happened next! Of course, as soon as I got back to the flat and the privacy of my room, I am tortured with guilt that I should not be going out with another man and I should not have enjoyed myself.

On Monday there was a bit of a buzz in the back office but as I was busy with planning for a training course, I did not find out what it was about until later in the day. It turns out that Chris, who has been working in Scotland, has decided she would prefer to work there permanently. This is because her boyfriend lives in Edinburgh and to be honest, I can't blame her for that. It is a problem for our Wimbledon office though, because it leaves quite an additional workload for the remaining staff.

I did not give this any more thought as it does not affect me. When Paul and Iris asked if they could speak with me at the end of the day, I was not really prepared for what came next.

'How are you enjoying your job, Jane?' asked Paul.

'It's fine, thank you. I hope you are satisfied?' I responded with a smile.

'We are, Jane. However, I do wonder if you are a bit bored sometimes? We notice that once all the typing is done you come in to us to ask if there is anything else you can do,' said Iris. 'It is also quite evident to us that your organisational skills are impressive and you show quite a lot of insight into the wider work of the team.'

I was not sure how to respond to this. Was it a criticism or a compliment? Before I could react, Paul leapt in. 'The thing is, Jane, with Chris leaving we need to find a way to cover the workload. We wondered if you would be willing to take on more of an administrative role. With a salary increase, of course.'

This was actually quite a dilemma for me. First of all, I have a feeling that Florence and Sylvia will not like it, as it will be tantamount to the new girl being promoted from a junior role over their heads. Perhaps worse than that, I know from my job as a recruitment consultant in my real life, that you cannot just make up a new job and offer it someone you like, there does need to be an open and fair competition. You would think a trade union would be fully aware of this but their approach seemed to me to be a bit too laid back. If those were not real concerns, I was also conscious that sharing an office with Andy could create some tensions. All this flashed through my mind in milliseconds.

'Oh. That's a bit of a surprise. Well the idea is tempting but I would like to think about it please. I presume you will need time to draw up a job description and advertise the vacancy too? Could we talk about this again next week?'

Paul and Iris exchanged looks. 'Yes of course,' said Iris, 'although I think you have already demonstrated your suitability. You can help us draft the job spec next week and we will talk again then.'

At this point Andy returned to his desk. I have a feeling he had been asked to make himself scarce for a while. He was smiling quietly to himself and unless I was mistaken, I think he might have actually winked at me. I'm not used to flirting at work. I'm not complaining, it's just a bit strange.

'I'm heading off home now Andy, but I'll see you on Sunday about noon?'

Friday June 26th
June has been quite an eventful month what with Sue and Pete's wedding in the offing, Kate coming out quite discreetly to the others as well as planning to move in with Anne, the change of government which doesn't appear to have any impact yet and now a potential job change.

I am no nearer to finding my way back to my own time though. I did try checking out the pavement area where I think I tripped or at least it's the last place I remember being before waking up in 1970. No clues there.

The Sunday lunch with Anne and Andy was really relaxing. Angie and Sue cooked roast lamb with mint sauce and although there wasn't a lot to go round the six of us, the mixed vegetables were pleasant. I really don't understand the appeal of packet mashed potato – it's called Smash – but I think it is mimicking what the astronauts had on the Apollo 11 flight to the moon. I had been under the impression that man first stood on the moon years ago (well, it was as far as I was concerned) but I had not realised it was last year. The girls just laughed that I had "forgotten" something as historic as that. We had Artic Roll for dessert, which is also the height of fashion at the moment. It is ice cream wrapped in a sponge cake.

As Kate and I washed up and we could hear a gentle buzz of conversation about the General Election result and the tennis. Our flat is very near to the All England Lawn Tennis and Croquet Club and we are right in the middle of the Championships. The men's final will be played next Saturday. Strangely enough, although we live so close, none of us have ever been to watch a match. The whole thing is rather expensive, so we just open the windows and we can hear the applause every time someone gets a match point.

20. Summer Loving

I started my new job in July. I think Iris has dealt with my concerns about Sylvia and Florence not being happy about my promotion as not a word was said. I am continuing to work in the typing office but I have a separate in-tray as much of what I am now doing involves organising events and meetings, making phone calls and sending one-off letters. All this works quite well as I wasn't sure how being in the same office as the senior people would turn out, especially as I would be so close to Andy all day.

Sylvia and I were the delighted recipients of an IBM golfball typewriter each, as Florence's trial had proved so successful. I thought that I would ask about getting a photocopier for the office too, although that will have to wait until the end of the year as it would seem greedy to embark on another major expenditure straight away. Can I really be thinking about what might happen later this year when all I want is to be home with my real family? I did look into photocopiers, reading the glossy catalogues that arrived in the office and discovered that they could be rented. Joan has a friend whose office had one but apparently it was always breaking down. She thought perhaps the engineer was trying it on, as he liked to chat to one of the young women in that office.

The talk in the flat was all about holiday options that Kate and Angie were planning with their respective partners. Sue and Pete had booked a fortnight in Cornwall for their honeymoon and of course, wedding arrangements were at the forefront of everyone's minds. Andy had been invited and had accepted, so we were heading off to Liverpool at the end of the month.

There were two really dreadful plane crashes which made us all thankful that we were not flying anywhere on holiday. First, a Dan-Air flight crashed in Barcelona and 112 people were killed. The very next day an Air Canada plane crashed in Toronto with 109 lives lost.

In my own time, most of the budget airlines have closed down in the UK although many still operate across Europe where they are based now. The interim government in the UK made much of the "green travel strategy" which saw the end of anything that required aviation fuel and in fact holidays abroad are really only open to the very wealthy. Trying to get a visa even for a short break is just too much trouble and expense so it is not worth it. Tom and I take the boys to North Wales or the seaside when we can. We are planning a trip to Scotland soon. At least, we were.

Anyway, I'm here now and much as I would prefer to be back in my own time, I have to keep a brave face on it until I can figure out how to get back.

I am actually dithering around in front of my wardrobe as I am trying to decide what to wear to Sue and Pete's big day. The weather is forecast to be quite mild although there could be showers.

I'm quite taken with the concept of the 'shift dress' which is sleeveless and very light and comfortable for the summer. I bought two of them on my shopping expedition with Angie. On the other hand, it may be a bit too informal for a wedding.

In the end I settle on my long floaty dress which I think is suitably smart as well as pretty. I love it as I can wear it on other less formal occasions too. We will keep our fingers crossed for the weather. Andy has his work suit which will look just fine. We have booked our coach tickets and Sue has sorted out where we can stay. This will be with relatives of hers and it means that her uncle can pick us up from the bus station and drive us to the church, so we are all organised. Andy and I went into Elys yesterday to buy the wedding present. In the end we chose a tablecloth as it will be easier to carry on the coach journey than the Pyrex cookware we had originally thought of.

Angie has found a friend from work to take over Sue's flat when she moves out. I haven't met her yet but I'm sure she will be just fine. Even if the talk every evening revolves largely around happenings at Marks & Spencer!

We have not sorted out who will move into Kate's flat although she has already been emptying her belongings into Anne's big old van and some of the furniture will be going shortly. Andy has expressed an interest in moving in but I am truthfully unsure about that. For a start, it could change the dynamics in the house to have three women and one man, especially as two of us are in a relationship. Supposing we split up? Supposing any disagreement turns into an "us and them" or upstairs versus downstairs? Andy also does not seem to be too keen on the weekly cleaning rota and even less enthusiastic about the meals' rota. Every time I mention cooking, he suggests we should go back to San Lorenzo. That is fine, but it is neither a cheap nor an everyday option! So, I have stopped mentioning it for now in the hope that we can find another female for the flat. Don't get me wrong, in some ways it would be great to live next door to Andy and I'm very fond of him. To be honest "very fond" barely describes how I feel. It's just that under these circumstances I don't think it would work.

I have some leave owing shortly as my new job has an extra week's holiday allowance. I haven't decided how to use it but I am so relieved that I don't have to go to Canada to stay with relatives I don't know!

Andy has suggested that we should plan a week away together this summer in addition to the wedding trip. He is keen on camping but I am not really a fan. We have discussed various options but it is so difficult for me because when he asks if I have been somewhere before, I cannot say "yes but with my husband and children many years from now" so I have to pretend I have not been anywhere much. I think he is running out of patience with my vagueness.

I have already said that I need to find an opportunity for me to call in to see my parents at some stage this summer, although I am dreading that too. From my brief, rather one-sided telephone conversations with my mum I think she expects the amnesia to have gone by now so that she can chat with me about things relating to my growing up years. If we can't do that, which obviously is impossible, I don't know what we can talk about. They have not met Andy although I've told them I am going out with a friend from work but I am worried they will assume the relationship is an important one. Well, it is. But I don't want them to jump to conclusions.

Some days I scream silently to myself about the dilemma I am embroiled in. If I didn't love Tom so much it would be much more manageable. I cry when I think of Logan and Theo growing up without me. I just want to go home.

If I stopped spending time with Andy then at least I wouldn't feel guilty about my husband and children in quite the same way. On the other hand, I would still see Andy every day and everyone would want to know why I had rejected such a lovely guy.

Apart from this set of indecisions it has been a good summer so far. Work is quite interesting and I am slowly learning more about the trade union movement. When the weather is right, Andy and I go for some great local walks. The atmosphere in the flat is full of excitement and anticipation. Angie is coming to the end of her management course and is waiting to find out where she will be posted. Sue spends all her spare time dealing with wedding lists, trying to sort out friends and relations' travel and accommodation or on the phone to her mother. Kate has almost moved out but stays in the flat during the week.

I am still trying to make sense of what has happened to me. The best theory I can come up with so far is that there are parallel universes (I think it's called a multiverse, but I could have made that up!) and that somehow or other I have accidentally slipped between them. There is clearly a Jane who is quite similar to me in this universe but it would seem we took different paths. There could be lots more Janes too. In this particular one Jane is not married to Tom and does not have children. This Jane is living in 1970 but the Jane that is really me was living in 2027.

Whether any of that is logical I don't know. The other, most distressing part, is working out how I can get back to my own universe or whether I am stuck here for the rest of this Jane's life.

I have gone over and over what happened the day it all changed. I know that it was Friday 13th March and although I have no time for superstitions I sure as hell will be really careful the next time that date comes around. All I can remember was dropping the boys off at school and going to work to meet an important client. I cannot even remember his or her name now.

I have been confiding in my diary but I don't think it makes me feel much better. Several times I have wanted to tell someone but I think it most likely they will assume I am schizophrenic or that I have mental health problems. I do wonder what Andy would say. He is my closest friend right now and he is kind and thoughtful. I don't think the time is right at the moment, but maybe once we have known each other longer?

21. The Wedding

We are going to Sue and Pete's wedding tomorrow. We have both taken the afternoon off work in order to travel to the home of Sue's aunt and uncle who live nearby and have kindly agreed to put us up. The coach journey was a remarkably efficient way to travel and it occurs to me that a similar journey would have taken much longer in my own time – that's progress for you!

Sue's Uncle John was waiting at the bus station and in no time at all we were sitting in their tidy semi drinking tea and making polite conversation. Auntie Ruth was very kind although she did keep fussing around us, so I expect they don't have visitors often. Uncle John is a rather portly gentleman with a red face who puffs and blows as he walks. By contrast Auntie Ruth is tiny, almost bird-like in her mannerisms. They are retired, and I wouldn't be surprised if Sue's wedding was the most exciting thing to have happened to them for several years.

We sat talking about some of the things in the news today. Fortunately, Andy bought a newspaper earlier this morning and I'd studied it during the coach journey. I still cannot relax in case a subject comes up that I should have known about. For example, only the other day while I was in the back office there was a comment about "little weed". I wrongly assumed they were talking about marijuana but it turned out it was a character in a children's television programme from the 1950s called The Flower Pot Men. Bill and Ben were flower pot men who lived at the bottom of the garden, along with a sunflower called Little Weed. Everyone laughed at my mistake but it does little for my confidence when people expect me to know these things. Our discussion with Sue's aunt and uncle stayed on safer ground so that was good.

After a while, I asked if I could put my overnight bag in the bedroom and I was amused to notice that we were in a room with a single bed and a fold-up guest bed. Auntie Ruth was nervously flitting around until I said how much we appreciated them having us to stay and that we would be very comfortable. She confessed she was not sure if we were "just friends" which I think was a euphemism for asking whether we were sleeping together. I confirmed that the arrangement would be just fine, which of course did not answer her unspoken question.

As it turned out, we thought it wise to be as discreet as possible so although we had a lovely cuddle (that's all!) in the single bed that night, afterwards Andy took the flimsy bed and I enjoyed the comfort of the divan.

On my own in bed, I could not stop myself from thinking about my wedding day with Tom. It was exactly how we wanted it, with no fuss or unnecessary expense, just the two of us making our lifelong promises to each other. It was also quite an adventure to go to Scotland without letting our families know. Whilst I certainly wish Sue and Pete a very happy marriage, I am aware that they had been planning for this day and saving up for months. These things are of course a matter of personal choice and I drifted off to sleep imagining that I was back home with Tom and the boys.

I had assumed earlier that both Pete and Sue would be having some kind of hen/stag night celebrations as is the norm in my time. However, it seemed that Sue wanted to spend the evening at home with her sisters and parents and Pete was travelling up with his best man and not expecting to arrive until late.

The next morning, after breakfast, Sue called round to see us. She hinted that she needed to talk to me privately so we made the pretence of going out in the garden to admire Uncle John's roses. It transpired that Pete had inadvertently got himself in a bit of trouble when they arrived last night. He had met up with a few mates for a quiet drink which had got slightly out-of-hand. Pete had been arrested for stealing a beer glass from the pub. I imagine it had got a bit lively and the police had been called. He had spent the night in the police cells and was expected in court this morning.

I did my best to reassure Sue that it was unlikely that the magistrate would make too much of the incident under the circumstances and we should all carry on as if nothing had happened. She had not revealed to her family any of this and I think she just wanted someone to talk to. Hopefully my words will have had a calming effect as she went off to get her hair done looking more relaxed. Frankly, I have no idea whether he will make it to the church on time but I thought Sue really did not want her big day ruined by worrying about it.

Andy and I travelled to the church with Uncle John and Auntie Ruth and I must say I was massively relieved to see Pete arriving some ten minutes after us, none-the-worse for his ordeal. I gave him a discreet "thumbs-up" so I suppose he will realise that I was aware of the situation.

The flowers in the church were impressive. I had not realised that Ruth and John had arranged them themselves during yesterday afternoon, before Andy and I arrived to stay with them. Maybe I under-estimated the pair of them because I can now see that they had all been grown in Uncle John's garden and Auntie Ruth's floral displays were truly professional looking.

Once the church had filled up with family and friends, Sue arrived looking radiant. I think some of that glow was utter relief that Pete had turned up without further mishap. The church service followed the standard order of all wedding services with a couple of hymns and in no time at all Sue and Pete were exchanging their vows and entering into what we all hoped would be a very happy marriage.

Outside the church, the wedding photographer spent a lot of time arranging us to his satisfaction. Fortunately, it was warm so we didn't mind standing around. Weddings in my own time are much more likely to be captured on video including everything from the hen and stag parties (some of which can last over several weekends or involve expensive trips away). In fact, much of the effort goes into everything looking perfect for the video rather than concentrating on the purpose of the event. I rather liked the simplicity evident here of taking still photos of that moment in time when the bride and groom look at each other as if to say 'we've done it!'

Eventually everyone moved off to the reception which was being held in a hotel within walking distance. Again, I admired the practicality of these arrangements. It seemed much more intimate than coachloads of people being driven to a distant venue, although I suppose it would not have been so relaxing had it been pouring with rain.

Sue's efforts with the table plan were duly acknowledged as we were able to sit with the few people we already knew and a few that we got to know better over the course of the buffet. Kate and Anne sat opposite us, Angie and Rob beside us and a selection of family members, including Ruth and John filled the rest of the table. I haven't been to many weddings in my own time but I have found them uncomfortable if I do not know many guests, so this was actually quite enjoyable.

The conversation was rather everyday at the outset, with people commenting on the flowers, the vicar and the service, how lovely the bride looked etc. The hotel staff were efficiently laying out the food on some large trestle tables at the rear of the room.

I gave this hardly a glance until I saw something that brought me up short. One of the waiters, dressed in a white shirt, bow tie and black waistcoat, looked exactly like my husband Tom. His build was identical, his hair was dark with just the same floppy fringe. Oh Tom! It could not be! It was not possible! This was Birkenhead, near Liverpool, in 1970 not 2027. I could feel myself trembling.

I waited until the man returned with another tray of food and without realising what I was doing I stood up and lurched towards him. Andy was immediately aware of my sudden movement and called out, 'Hey, Jane. You can't have the food yet until they've done the speeches!' By the time I reached the table the waiter had gone and although I was tempted to follow him into the kitchen, I realised I could not do that without causing a scene. I tried to make it look like I was checking something on the floor for a few minutes but the waiter did not come out again.

Returning to my table just as Pete's Best Man tapped on his glass for quiet, I smiled at Andy as if nothing was wrong, although I have a feeling there were tears at the corners of my eyes. He gestured as if to say, 'Are you OK?' and I nodded.

While the speeches were being made, I hardly listened apart from laughing when everyone else did and applauding on cue. I was too busy trying to make sense of what I saw. I am certain it was Tom, but there is no way I can explain it to myself or anyone else for that matter. Perhaps I so much wanted to see him and be with him that I imagined it? It's over four months since I last saw my beloved husband but he's never far from my thoughts.

Finally, after the cake was cut and the bride and groom invited everyone to help themselves from the buffet, Andy turned to me. 'What was that about? Were you really that hungry?'

I was at a complete loss to come up with a rational explanation. Finally, I concluded I would have to tell the truth, or at least a version of it. 'I know it will sound strange Andy, but I thought I saw someone that I knew, a long time ago. I must have been mistaken.'

Andy shook his head, rather mystified. 'He must have been someone rather special for you to dash off like that. You were faster than a speeding bullet.'

I smiled and shrugged, trying to imply that it wasn't worth discussing further. 'Let's get some of that lovely food and a piece of wedding cake for luck.'

The rest of the reception passed off without any further appearance of Tom and I convinced myself that I had imagined it. Just for a moment, when Andy asked me to dance, I shivered to think my husband could be watching me with another man. Andy's kiss at the end of the evening was tempered by that thought too. I decided I must put the incident out of my head if I am to settle in the world I find myself in.

22. Holiday

'Good morning my lovely Jane!' Andy bounded into the office with this happy greeting. Fortunately, neither Florence nor Sylvia were in yet, otherwise I would be in for some criticism.

'Hi Andy. You're sounding cheerful today! Any reason for that or is it just because the sun is shining?'

'Well, I hope you are going to like this but I've managed to get two tickets for the Isle of Wight music festival later this month! My mate Rob bought them but he cannot use them now. What do you think?'

'It sounds like fun. I've never been to the Isle of Wight and I don't know much about the music festival. What's it like?'

'It starts on a Wednesday and runs until the Sunday. I thought we could go early, say during the weekend, set up our tent, see a bit of the island and then enjoy the music. There are some great bands appearing including The Who and The Doors,' exclaimed Andy, almost breathless with excitement.

I have heard of some of these musicians on the radio, or watching Top of the Pops and hearing my flatmates discuss what is good and what is not. I thought a week away under canvas was the last thing I wanted to do but as Andy was so thrilled about the possibility, I would go along willingly. I do like to try different things.

'I think it might be a good idea to fit in a brief visit to see my parents before our trip away then.'

'Fine. Can I come with you?'

I wasn't expecting that, but it would be nice to have some company.

That evening I had a search around the bedroom and discovered a sleeping bag on top of the wardrobe. It was made of cotton and stuffed with kapok, covered in red tartan, in other words hardly the sort of thing I would use in my real life. It did not smell stale or unpleasant and I concluded it would do the job especially as Andy had a tent. Given that I was expecting this to be my one and only experiment with camping it didn't seem worth spending any money on buying anything new.

Kate tapped on the door gently. 'Hi, are you busy?'

'Not really, Kate. I am sorting out some things for a camping trip Andy is organising for us to the Isle of Wight. It's a music festival.'

'Wow. That's amazing. I read about that in Time Out, it's supposed to be really good.'

'Can I help with something?'

'I'm trying to move a cupboard and I think it's a two-person job.

One way and another, moving the cupboard, discussing Kate's move, having a cup of tea together and sorting through Kate's clothes took the rest of the evening. It was useful though as Kate had an old rucksack which she gave to me, which will come in handy for the Isle of Wight.

I have just phoned my mum – it is always mum who answers the phone – and asked if it would be convenient for Andy and I to go over for lunch this coming Saturday. She was delighted and I was glad that I had asked.

At work the next morning, Andy was out but he had clearly been in very early to collect papers for a meeting or something. He left a note on my desk.

Jane. Really sorry but I cannot make it this weekend to meet your parents. Will tell you more later. Andy xx

I sighed to myself. It didn't really matter but I was looking forward to Andy's company and I thought he would be a helpful foil against my mum's questions. I am wondering if he has got cold feet about meeting my parents. If only we had mobile phones, we could have discussed this immediately or texted a quick message. As it is, I'm not sure when he is back in the office. So now I will have to phone mum again tonight to tell her not to cook too much!

23. Family visit

I have heard nothing from Andy this week and he has not been in the office at all. This morning I got the tube into central London and the metropolitan line out to Uxbridge. It was quite a long journey, but I enjoyed the views on the occasional over ground sections and I have been reading my book for the rest of the journey. It is 'Future Shock' by Alvin Toffler. It is about the speed of change in technology and in society. It's very interesting but honestly, if the author had any idea of how much life would have changed by my time, he would be amazed. In the light of what I have been reading, I guess it is not surprising how challenging it has been for me to adapt to an earlier age.

I am also reading 'What color is your parachute?' by Richard Bolles. He's an American so the spelling is American English which is a bit irritating. He writes about career planning and how to find a job. As you can imagine, that is very relevant to work in my real life and I am still trying to believe that I will get back to my own time. Although I am enjoying both books, I really wish I could have downloaded them on my Kindle like in my real life. It's so much easier to refer back to things later, rather than trying to flick through paper pages to find something. Even worse, paperbacks are so heavy to carry compared to an e-reader.

I bought a cyclamen in a pot to give to my mother and as I have no idea what sort of flowers she likes, I'm hoping it will be acceptable. It is truly awkward to carry on the train along with my two books.

Before long, I arrive at my imposter parents' house. I shouldn't really call them that, as they are as genuine as they could be. It's me that is in the wrong place and time. I've been dreading this visit as it's sure to be really tricky because I cannot ask where everything is (such as the toilet) given that I'm supposed to have grown up there. Mum opens the door with a big smile. Before I have a chance to sit down, I thank her for bringing the bag of goodies to the flat to help jog my memory and she says I can go up to my room to see if there's anything else that I want.

I venture up the stairs and fortunately it is fairly obvious which was my childhood bedroom. I think the pink flowery curtains and matching bedspread are a give-away. I suppose people didn't have duvets in those days. I cannot imagine having to grow up with that sort of pink ditsy kind of stuff but of course, in those days it was always "pink for a girl, blue for a boy"! It is strange to look round this room as if I had slept there all throughout my childhood. Nothing looks familiar to me, but why would it as I actually grew up in the noughties. I also spot which is the bathroom so I can begin to relax. I look around the room and notice one or two ornaments. Mum appears behind me. 'Can I have these?' I say, pointing to two china ballerinas. 'Of course you can!' she replies, 'I was always sorry that you refused to take anything from home when you moved out.'

'Well, I am a little bit more thoughtful now,' I say, hoping not to make life difficult by saying so. We go downstairs together and I find that I am beginning to like her.

'Thank you for the cyclamen,' she says. 'How lovely you remembering that it was grandad's favourite flower!'

Just as I'm trying to work out how to handle this disturbing revelation, Dad appears, wiping his hands on a grubby-looking cloth. He has been doing something to their car, changing the oil, I think. I am still getting my head round the fact that everyone still uses petrol or diesel motors. I didn't know that people did their own car repairs and servicing either but I suppose it is a habit from having to be more self-sufficient during and after the second world war. 'Do you want any help, Dad?' I say. He beams with delight. 'I could do with someone to find a nut and bolt I have dropped somewhere,' he says. We both go back to the garage and within seconds I have spotted it. 'There you are!'

'Thank you, Jane. You always were a good little helper!'

Lunch was quite enjoyable too. Mum had cooked a chicken casserole with fresh vegetables from the garden. I found the dessert, which was a treacle tart with desiccated coconut, much too sweet for my twenty-first century palate but I managed to eat it anyway.

I used the opportunity of my visit to tell them about the plans for the summer. They were pleased to hear about Sue and Pete's wedding and I also told them that Andy and I were going camping on the Isle of Wight. I didn't mention that it was a music festival nor that I had not heard from him since Monday. They were interested to know if my friendship with Andy was "serious" and I tried to give as honest an answer as possible, saying that we worked together and I enjoyed his company. I did explain why I had given up teaching because of the amnesia and they seemed to understand.

Before long, it was time for me to get back to the station for the long journey back. My mum's last words were quite telling: 'It's been lovely to see you, Jane. You may have had a nasty accident which has changed you quite a lot, but we love you anyway.'

That went a long way towards me feeling less of an imposter in my parents' house and more at home in 1970 than I ever expected to be.

24. Is it over?

There was no news from Andy on Sunday and I was beginning to think he did not want to see me anymore. I went for a quiet solo walk on the Common. Everyone else in the flat was busy with their own things and I felt really lonely, not for the first time. I've spent a lot of time worrying about how Tom and the boys are coping without me. I even worried if Dog was missing me too. Oh, I so wish I could go home and find that everything is just the way I left it. I am utterly frustrated by not being able to do anything about my situation.

Still no contact from Andy and by Monday morning I was wondering how to deal with what seemed to be the abrupt end of my relationship. By mid-morning I went in to the back office with some completed work for Paul. Iris asked if I had any news. I wasn't quite sure what she meant and I must have looked more than usually absent-minded.

'Paul, did you give Jane the message from Andy last week?' she said. Paul clapped his hand to his face, suddenly cringing with embarrassment.

'Jane. I'm so sorry, it must have slipped my mind.'

'What's all this about then?' I asked.

'Andy's mother was taken ill and he had to go up north to see her. I think it was a heart attack; it was something serious.'

'Hasn't anybody heard from him then?'

'It would seem not.'

I went back to my desk, full of concern and worry. I tried to concentrate on my work but I wasn't making a very good job of it. How selfish of me to think that it was anything to do with me when in fact Andy's mother could be fighting for her life. I felt quite ashamed.

Around lunchtime, Joan signalled to me through the glass panel that separated the reception area and the typists' room. 'I've got a phone call for you, Jane. I think it might be Andy but his voice is rather faint. Shall I put it through upstairs so you can be private?'

I nodded my agreement while striding upstairs two steps at a time. Bless you Joan, when the chips are down you can be relied on to be discreet.

'Hello. Andy?'

'Hello Jane. I'm sorry I haven't been able to keep in touch it's been all rather fraught here. Did you get my message?'

'Not until this morning I'm afraid. It slipped Paul's mind.'

'Oh no. What a numbskull he is. Well, the good news is that my mum is pulling through after a few worrying days and I hope to be back in London in a day or two. I'm sorry I missed meeting your parents though.'

'Oh Andy, that doesn't matter now. I'm so pleased your mum is improving. Please give her my best wishes and tell her that I look forward to meeting her in due course. My Mum and Dad were sorry not to meet you but there will be other occasions. You just look after yourself and I shall be delighted to see you when you get back.'

'Thanks, my lovely lady. This has to be a short chat because I'm on the hospital pay phone and I'm running out of coins. I've had to call various family members over the week in case Mum didn't survive. I didn't want to phone you until I had some positive news. See you soon. 'Bye my love.'

I put the phone down amidst a range of emotions. He called me 'my love'. I had actually been more worried than I had realised and I felt like crying with some relief. Instead, I walked slowly down the stairs while I composed myself and thanked Joan for enabling me to take the call in private. I then went into the back office and gave Iris and Paul an abbreviated version of the news from Andy, before getting on with the day's work with a much lighter heart.

This episode caused me to think long and hard about my priorities in this strange new world. Much as I yearn to be back with Tom and the boys, it may never happen. I could be here for ever.

I'm enjoying my job although the world of work is very different here in 1970. It was reported on the radio recently that over ten million working days have been lost through strike action, already this year. Some of the strikes are not even supported by any trade union although most notably nurses and electricity company workers are considered by the general public to be justifiable.

It seems that the introduction of new technology – relative to what existed previously – is reducing the number of jobs. The level of redundancies is a real worry and we are one of the trade unions that is working hard to retrain people when their work is automated, and their jobs disappear. Meanwhile, employers are trying to save money by cutting jobs and urging their remaining workers to increase their productivity. Add to the mix the fact that there are many shop stewards who are more than happy to stir up trouble. Often, our full-time officials can do little about this.

A couple of years ago a government White Paper called "In Place of Strife", produced by Barbara Castle, a Member of Parliament, tried to establish things like having a ballot before a strike takes place as well as a 28-day cooling off period. It was not implemented and so my colleagues continue to tread a difficult line between enabling shop stewards to improve working conditions and supporting members who are being badly treated by their employers.

Haven't I learned a lot! Of course, much of this is discussed in the back office. I don't join in, but I do listen!

Andy discusses some of these things with me as well. I have to be very careful not to appear shocked at some of the things I hear and equally recognise that some of my own thoughts really only fit the economic situation of my own time in the twenty-first century.

So, for now, I am doing my best to fit in with the life I have found myself in. I am relieved that Andy's mum is on the mend. I look forward to seeing him as soon as possible too.

25. Isle of Wight

I'm feeling just a bit excited about my impending holiday, despite the camping dimension! I've packed the small rucksack that Kate has given me with the bare minimum of clothes. Basically, shorts, a couple of tee-shirts, a summer shift dress and my best long skirt as well as a jumper and waterproof jacket which I hope will cover all eventualities. I asked the others what to wear to a music festival and no one seemed have much idea.

I'm looking forward to time off work and to spending it with Andy. I would much rather be with Tom and the boys and I feel dreadfully guilty even to be anticipating this short break with Andy. I keep trying to tell myself that we are just good friends. Sometimes I think I should just tell him I am married and make up some story as to why my husband and children are not here. But then I would have to explain the same thing to Kate, Sue and Angie and everyone at work and they would realise that I have lied to them and anyway, it would not fit with what they know. Oh, I'm so confused. If there was even the slightest opportunity of getting back to my real life I would jump at the chance. I would give anything for my life to go back to how it was. At night, if I am not crying, I am lying awake thinking of my beloved family. I cannot find anything to give me any hope though.

The truth is, that even when I am enjoying myself, I feel guilty. I would not dream of being unfaithful to Tom and yet here I am planning to go on holiday with another man. Oh, I wish life wasn't so complicated.

Anyway, it is what it is and we plan to set off early this morning, so I've set the alarm to be ready for when Andy arrives at the flat.

Last week we had a discussion, or perhaps I should say argument, about how to travel to the festival. Andy suggested hitch-hiking. I know they used to do this in the past, but I consider it to be dangerous in so many ways. Apart from anything else, it is extremely inefficient unless you happen to be lucky and find someone planning to go to the exact same place otherwise you could end up zig-zagging across the country and possibly never getting to your intended destination. Then you don't know who is giving you a lift and whether they are perverts or prone to unprovoked violence! I thought it was against the law to hitch-hike but as I'm not sure about this I didn't want to risk stirring up even further disagreement. I could not, of course, use as evidence how relatively inexpensive public transport is compared with the twenty-first century that I am used to, but I did eventually convince Andy that when we took the coach to Sue and Pete's wedding it worked out fine.

So here we are on the underground, heading for Victoria. Andy seems heavily laden with the tent and everything he thinks we might need for over a week away. I feel relatively unprepared but, to be honest, even in my own time I travel light.

Victoria bus station is extremely busy, and I am afraid we might not be able to get tickets. We are getting a United bus to Southampton, then a Red Funnel ferry to the Isle of Wight. I'm not sure what happens after that.

Well, we did get seats eventually, but I really wish they were not next to the toilet cubicle. We seem to be enveloped by a pervading smell of urine which I presume is occasioned by the male visitors to our part of the coach not managing to stay upright while the coach swerves round corners. There are worse smells later in the journey and any foolish idea that we might eat the sandwiches I have made carefully, has gone straight out of the proverbial window. To be honest, a window for some fresh air might not be a bad thing. I have already admitted to Andy that hitchhiking might have been more enjoyable.

Finally, the coach has arrived at Southampton and we now have to walk to the ferry terminal. I'm really tired but appreciating the fresh air. My rucksack is weighing heavily on my shoulders. Goodness knows how Andy is managing with the tent and cooking stuff in his.

It was a long wait for the ferry but at least we could see it coming across the sea. It took another age for the passengers to get off. There are a few other people in the queue also here early for the festival so there is much chat about such as which bands might be playing and where it's best to camp.

The ferry crossing was smooth and there was a pleasant breeze so I am starting to enjoy myself. Apparently, we have to get a bus to the farm where the festival is being set up. Another long wait for a bus. Some of the others decided to hitch, but I will admit to just a teeny-weeny smile of satisfaction when we saw them still walking as we passed them on the bus, half an hour later.

The bus driver did not seem too well informed about the festival so he dropped us near a field which he reckoned was a good place to camp. We couldn't find a farmer to ask permission but, in the end, we decided to set up the tent here anyway.

It's funny, at work Andy is quiet and relatively easy-going, but I have to be honest and admit that he's not the best tempered when something doesn't go his way. By that I mean putting up a tent. I thought, erroneously, that as camping was his "thing" that he would know how to erect a tent even though it has started to rain and it's quite breezy on this cliff-top. It probably hasn't helped that I got a fit of the giggles.

'For heaven's sake, Jane, come and do something useful like hold this guy line!' he exploded a minute or two ago, as the thing almost got away from him. Yes, I know it would be disastrous if it blew away but honestly it was really funny just seeing him battle with the unruly heap of canvas and rope.

Unlike tents in my own time (did I mention that I don't like camping?) which have a sewn-in ground sheet and a bendy frame which requires a mere shake to put it in position, this monstrosity involved pegging out a heavy canvas, fixing together bamboo poles and threading them through sleeves in the tent wall then anchoring the whole in rock-hard soil without anything to hammer in the metal pegs, and then trying to lay a separate waterproof sheet down while the breeze stiffened into storm force. Well, I might be exaggerating a bit there but you get the picture.

Finally, the tent was in place and our tempers were similarly frayed but intact.

'I've brought something for our tea but to be honest I don't really feel like cooking,' observed Andy as the sky darkened.

'You see that light over there,' I pointed, 'do you think it might be worth checking it out? It could be a pub and it can't be more than a ten-minute walk.'

We set off across the field, which turned out to be much muddier than I had expected. As we got closer, we could see it really was a pub. Even more exciting, it was open!

'We can ask if we can camp here anyway,' said Andy. 'Might even get a pint.'

I can't tell you what a joy it was to open that door and be greeted by a friendly murmur of local voices. There was an elderly gentleman sitting at the bar who entreated us to shut the door and come in. The landlady, wearing an old-fashioned cross-over apron, smiled immediately and asked what we would have to drink. Across the room were four more beer drinkers deep in conversation about livestock. Although it is late August and hardly necessary for heating purposes, the wood fire blazing at the back of the room made the whole scene relaxing.

Andy, polite as ever, asked me what I would like to drink before enquiring if we would be allowed to camp in the field. We were told it was no problem as long as we didn't leave any rubbish and there would be no charge. Things are starting to look up, I thought.

The landlady was able to offer us a home-made steak and ale pie, boiled potatoes and peas. It was delicious. Little did we know that it would be the last proper meal for nearly a week!

It turned out that we had come to the wrong farm and the place where the festival was being held was Afton Down, several miles away. Looking at my downcast expression, Jack, one of the locals said that if we were up and packed by six-thirty the next morning, he would give us a lift to the correct location. The thought of dismantling that wretched tent in the early hours was not inspiring, but it was such a kind offer we could not refuse.

Amazingly, I slept like a log, no doubt helped by the cosy bar, the beer and the tasty meal.

When I woke, Andy was already stuffing his sleeping bag into his rucksack and tucking odds and ends into the side pockets. I took somewhat longer to wake up and Andy was doing everything he could to hurry me up. 'Come on, sleepyhead we need to be ready in fifteen minutes!' he urged.

Dismantling the tent was almost as chaotic as putting it up but somehow or other we were just doing a last check round to make sure we hadn't left anything when our friend of the night before was in the lane and tooting his horn.

I've never had a ride on a tractor before and I'm hoping it will be a one-off experience. In any case, we were grateful for the lift and it was actually quite interesting to see over the hedges at any on-coming traffic that was bowling along too fast to avoid us on these single-track roads.

Jack dropped us off at what he said would be the entrance to the music festival. He seemed quite sure that we were in the right place or at least where the festival had been held in two previous years.

We strolled across the fields towards where there were several people gathered. We guessed that they were roadies for one of the bands due to play but they did not seem at all busy.

'Hi' said Andy, 'does anyone know where the festival is being held?' 'No. Are you one of the organisers?' asked one of the group, who could have been a well-known musician for all we knew.

We stood around for a while wondering what to do next and as nothing was happening, we decided we could erect the tent and then go for a walk to find breakfast. Just as we were debating where to pitch the tent a large truck arrived full of scaffolding. It was the first sign of activity we had seen for some time and we concluded that if the metal poles were the makings of a stage, then that would at least give us some idea of the festival layout. Shortly after a man came running across the field to ask us what we were doing. We explained that we were here for the music festival and, rather rudely I thought, he laughed at us. 'You don't want to camp this close to the stage!' he commented. 'There will be thousands of people here. You'd be better off behind that hedge.' He pointed to a field some distance away, so we thanked him and with little confidence in his suggestion, headed that way.

In the absence of any better proposal we started to lay out the tent. This time I was able to hand the poles to Andy and together we made a better job of it. It only took us half an hour, by which stage we were really hungry.

'Let's see what's around,' I said, wandering off in what looked like a promising direction. Twenty minutes later we concluded there was little that way apart from more farms and fields. By the time we got back to "our" field there was a distinct sense that things were being set up.

Andy walked over to the two men who appeared to be in charge to ask if they could suggest where we could get breakfast. Again, we had a feeling we were being laughed at but at least they were able to tell us where a bus stop was.

Finally, our luck changed. As we approached the bus stop, which was next to a wooden shelter, a bus appeared and we were able to jump on board. The driver said he would drop us near a cafeteria, so things were improving.

After a bumpy twenty-minute drive, which seemed to meander all over the neighbourhood, we arrived at 'The Lobster Pot'. I have a feeling that lobsters were not likely to be on the menu but Mary – as she was called, according to her necklace – was willing to get us a bacon butty and a pot of tea.

Thus, refreshed and ready for what was left of the day, we wandered around the village and made use of the public toilets. We did ask Mary if we were near any of the sights but she seemed unaware of any local attractions we could visit. A small grocery shop seemed to be all that was on offer, so we called in for some provisions before standing forlornly at the bus stop. The home-made pasties looked appetising so we bought four of those.

So far, our holiday was proving to be a disappointment but I was at least thankful that it was not raining. In fact, the weather seemed set fair for the forthcoming weekend. We spent the evening eating our pasties and playing card games by torchlight.

Tucked up in my sleeping bag I had another spasm of guilt. If Tom could see me now, he would be heartbroken. Would he understand that I am lonely? Would he know that I am missing him dreadfully? I really don't know what to do.

During the night there appeared to be some noisy goings-on but it wasn't until the morning that we discovered a small caravan was parked at the other side of the field, along with five tents of assorted shapes and sizes.

Just as I was creeping off to find a bush or wall to "spend a penny" behind, one of the new arrivals hurried over to speak to me. 'Hi. I'm Ian. Wendy and I are here for the festival, along with a few mates. Is it OK to camp here?'

'Oh hello. I'm Jane. We've been here a couple of days and it seems to be alright.'

'It's just that they made a bit of fuss at the gates about our caravan,' he said.

I must have looked puzzled but when I looked round the field properly, I could see that a team of people had been busy putting up corrugated iron fencing. I asked Ian where the gate was and he pointed some distance away.

'I had no idea. There wasn't a gate when we arrived! Mind you, we were directed to this area of the field by someone who seemed to know what he was talking about. You haven't seen any toilets, have you?'

Ian shook his head but smiled. 'You are welcome to use ours. It's in the caravan and I'll introduce you to Wendy.'

Somehow or other, after using their portable toilet, meeting Wendy and calling Andy over to do the same it felt as if we had known them for years. They and their friends, who were staying in the adjacent tents, were all from the West Midlands, Wolverhampton, I think.

We were just heading back to our own tent when a horde of people got off the bus and ambled into "our" field. Friendly greetings were called and more tents were put into place.

Suddenly an ear-splitting sound ricocheted across the valley: 'One. Two. One. Two. Testing. One. Two.' We all grinned at each other as it was evident that one of the early bands was setting up.

As the day progressed, we could see people streaming through the gate, each time the ferry disgorged its occupants.

There was more activity around the whole area, with vans arriving with equipment and musicians. It seemed that there was no overall co-ordination and whichever band had the most efficient roadies, they got to play first. Today we saw Jethro Tull and Ten Years After. Donovan was supposed to be on but either we missed him or he didn't turn up.

The whole event seemed dreadfully disorganised but who was I to criticise, having never been to a music festival before? Wendy and Ian had been here last year and they gave me a quick run-down. They had bought tickets in advance, as we had, but they were aware that there were many people who believed it should be a free festival. The idea is that anyone who wants to be here can be here; it's a kind of backlash against authority. I was afraid I would feel like a fish out of water but as the day went on, everything got relaxed. That might have been because so many people were out of their heads on drugs. It was quite funny really as they just wandered around with wild flowers in their headbands that they had picked from the surrounding fields. Everyone smiled at everyone else and greeted each other with "Hi man" or "peace and love" and "far out"!

I wondered what Andy's response to the drug-taking would be but I needn't have worried. 'Do you want to do any of that stuff?' he asked.

'Not really Andy. I'm having a good time without it.' He grinned and gave me a hug and that was all that was said on the subject. Mind you, there was so much around I suspect just breathing in around some of the musicians would have given us a moderate high!

That evening we had a rather strange and deeply worrying conversation. Andy asked me what hopes I had for the future. I really could not find any words to answer him. He wanted to know if I liked being with him. In the end I said that he was a good friend and that I did enjoy his company but I preferred not to make any plans for the future until my memory returned and my amnesia cleared. This clearly wasn't what he wanted to hear.

The next morning, he seemed rather quiet and pensive. He went for a walk on his own and later came back with a present for me. It was an Isle of Wight festival tee-shirt. He made some comment about "that will have to do for now". I felt rather sick because it is evident he has committed rather more to our relationship than I have, not surprisingly

– given my circumstances. I tried to make light of it all but I now know that I will have to address this before too long.

Every day at the festival brought new interest in the shape of bands I had never heard of, along with others that were really well known. The music was great although the practical arrangements were still very chaotic. Ian and Wendy were happy to let us use their toilet as there didn't seem to be any laid on. I have no idea where they emptied it but thought it best not to ask. Similarly, food provision was patchy so we made do with what we had with us, supplemented with snacks from the hot dog van when they had some available and cans of beer when they didn't.

The next day we saw Miles Davis, The Doors and Emerson Lake & Palmer as well as Joni Mitchell and Leonard Cohen. It was a great day, and still people were pouring in through the gates. There was some speculation as to how many people were here. I've never been to anything like it but it was clearly thousands and thousands.

Each day we wandered around until we could see crowds gathering somewhere and we would head off in that direction, asking people we met who was playing. There didn't seem to be any public address system so it was all very casual.

Highlights for me were Free, Chicago and Jimi Hendrix – but more of that later. Andy was thrilled to see The Who and the Moody Blues and we congratulated each other on our eclectic music tastes. To be honest, we didn't get much sleep but at least camping went up in my estimation, once one got used to the lack of facilities.

From time to time I wondered what it would have been like to be at this festival with Tom. In my real life we rarely do anything separately because we actually enjoy each other's company.

Ian and Wendy's friends said that there was a bit of trouble with people pulling down the fences and that the organisers had caved in and let people get in free. I thought that was a shame but didn't say anything.

On our last day, Andy and I discussed our plans for getting home. We realised that with the thousands and thousands of people there, it would be difficult to get off the island. We decided to leave very early the next morning and hope that we could get a bus back to the ferry. I was certain this would involve queuing for hours. As it happened, the last to come on stage was Jimi Hendrix.

I really wanted to see him but it seemed there were numerous delays because the previous bands were running late and his roadies had problems getting his sound system going. We were heading back to our tent, having said goodbye to our new friends, when suddenly he started up. It was well after midnight but I took one look at Andy and we turned around in order to make the most of our trip.

I should mention here that I have a vague memory from my real life, that Jimi Hendrix died not long after this festival, of a drugs overdose. I cannot be sure and without Wikipedia to check, I just don't know. It blew my mind (see, I'm fitting in with the people here already) to think I could have just touched him on the foot from our vantage point by the stage and said, "Hey Jimi - take it easy on the drugs, mate – you never know what that stuff is doing to you." As it was, I just enjoyed his music. Hendrix was truly amazing and it is evident he has a unique talent. He played well into the early hours so we had very little sleep.

The next morning, Andy was awake and packing up everything as it was getting light. There were people sleeping all over the place but few were up and ready to leave at the time we were quietly dismantling the tent. We concluded that there would not be any buses for ages as we headed towards the nearest bus stop. I was wearing my sturdiest shoes in preparation for a long walk when a minibus stopped next to us and asked if we wanted a lift to the ferry terminal. Did we! You bet. That was so kind of them and in a matter of minutes we were at the ferry terminal ready to wait for the earliest crossing.

The journey back was a nightmare. We had to wait hours to get on the ferry even though we had tickets. That meant we missed the coach to London from Southampton that we were booked on but fortunately they laid on some extra ones so we got home eventually. As it's bank holiday there were fewer trains from Victoria – mad isn't it? It's been great, but I'm really, really tired now.

Monday August 31st
Now I am back in the flat I am having serious concerns about what to do next about Andy. I am, after all, married. I am not free to let my relationship with him develop any further. It would be tantamount to bigamy.

The truth is that I have given up all hope that I can get back to my real life with Tom and the children and so to some extent I have pretended that my former life doesn't exist.

I feel so guilty that I've got myself in this pickle. It's not fair to Andy either who sees me as "a hard-working secretary sharing a flat with girlfriends, attractive and sensible with a delightful sense of humour". How is he to know about my confusing background?

I really, really like Andy. Under other circumstances I might go as far as to say that I love him. I also love my husband Tom, Logan and Theo and I would rather be with them in my own time.

I can see that this will be another night of tears and worry as I cannot put off dealing with my dilemma.

When Andy walked me to the flat this afternoon, he gave me a hug and kiss and said how much he would miss me until we get together again. He is going up to see his mum tomorrow so we will catch up with each other next weekend.

26. The Dilemma

I know that I cannot leave Andy's question hanging in the air. He's a good man and he deserves a thoughtful response. I've done nothing but think about it since I got back. In fact, I've been awake most of the night. I'm feeling half dead as a result.

On the one hand, I surely cannot agree to let our relationship develop any further as I know that I am married to Tom and that would be wrong.

On the other hand, if I am never able to return to my home and life in the twenty-first century then I do not want to remain unattached for the rest of my life.

If these complications did not exist, would I marry Andy? I like him very, very much, I enjoy his company, he is kind and funny and sensitive. Would I want to stay with him for ever? Would I have his children? Or am I just feeling broody because the others in the flat are getting settled?

I have said I will meet him in the coffee shop next to the office when he gets back from seeing his parents later this morning, so I shall have to have my answer ready for then.

'Jane! I'm just off now. Will you let the boiler engineer in, please?'

'See you later, Angie. By the way, what time is the man due?'

'They said he would be here by ten. Thanks. 'Bye.'

The door slammed as Angie hurried off to something important.

I looked at the clock and noticed it was already ten past ten. I am actually all ready to go out and Andy will be at the coffee shop by eleven.

Having been awake the whole night I have made my decision. I will leave behind my old life and live my new life to the full. I will take it very slowly but I am ready to move forward with Andy. I will never, ever get over the loss of my first and only real love and my children. There is no way I can find out what has happened to them in my absence, if that is what it is. But I realise that I cannot carry on living half in the present and half in the future. I have decided to dispose of that old notebook I have been using to confide my thoughts.

I go to the window to look out for the boiler man and I'm relieved to see the blue and white gas company van pull up outside our house. I let him in, show him the boiler which is actually the Ewart water heater which sits over the kitchen sink. I leave him to it.

It takes very little time to burn the pages of my notebook in the empty fireplace and in some way, I feel quite relieved by this action. I have to stop worrying about what is happening in my old world and move forward.

I check my hair, makeup and clothes. It has not taken me long to fit into this time. My blue denim jeans are all the rage and look good with my yellow Isle of Wight tee-shirt. My hair is back to its sleek, shiny, nearly blonde self, courtesy of the sunshine we experienced while we were away.

I pop into the kitchen to see the boiler man. Much as I could have predicted, he has lit a cigarette and is puffing on it thoughtfully. 'How's it coming on?' I ask.

'Well, it needs a new diaphragm so I'll have a look in the van in a minute to see if I've got one with me. Otherwise I will have to come back next week.'

I sigh audibly. We just want the job done now as we need the hot water to wash up. It is tedious having to boil kettles, to say the least. The problem is, I don't want to hang around and keep Andy waiting. Not for the first time I really wish mobile phones had been invented so I could just text Andy to say I might be late.

Eventually, the man finishes the job and I sign his job sheet to confirm we are happy that the problem is resolved. By this stage I am close to screaming with frustration as it is now ten-fifty. Hopefully Andy will get himself a coffee and read the paper while he waits for me.

As I hurry off down the road, I have a strange sense of déjà vu although I cannot quite put my finger on what this reminds me of. I almost break into a trot as I pass the Girls' School and by the time I am in the High Street I am checking my watch every couple of minutes.

I am feeling a bit light-headed, in fact the lack of sleep last night has made me feel dizzy, so I pause next to the seat by the railway station. I suppose it's because I have been stressing over the situation with Andy. I will just sit down and shut my eyes for a minute to see if I can clear my head and stop the world spinning round.

27. And then....

'Jane. Jane. Are you alright?' It was one of the other mothers at school.

'Sorry. I felt dizzy for a moment, so I thought I'd sit down.'

'Well I'm not surprised the speed you dash around. I presume you were coming to help with the vintage jumble sale?'

'Oh. Oh. Where am I? What day is it?'

'Saturday. You do look rather pale, Jane. I think you had better sit there a bit longer. Shall I get you a glass of water or would you like someone to go home with you?'

'No thank you. I will be OK soon. I am sorry, but I don't feel up to helping with the jumble sale. I think I should make my way home though.'

I feel quite faint and wobbly and I can hardly dare to believe that what I have been longing for these past months is actually happening.

As I approach 14 Viney Hill I am tentatively thrilled to see the neatly trimmed hedge, the wooden gate and the gleaming white uPVC windows. I don't use a key so I approach slowly, hoping that the electronic sensor will announce my presence.

A disembodied voice speaks. It is Tom. My Tom. 'Hello, Jane. You're back early!'

'Where are you, Tom?'

'Just dropping the boys off at Mum's. I thought you knew I was doing that while you were at the jumble sale.'

'Can you come home, please?'

'Is something wrong?'

'No, my darling. Everything is very, very right. I can't wait to see you!'

Tears stream down my face with relief as I am guessing I must be back home in my own time. Ten minutes later Tom strides up the road with a smile on his handsome face.

'Well, I can see you wasted no time at the vintage jumble sale. That tee-shirt is amazing!'

I look down and notice that I am still wearing the Isle of Wight tee-shirt that Andy bought me.

This has all taken place so suddenly I am not sure how to react. I give Tom an enormous hug and start crying again with relief. Poor man, he's totally confused. 'Whatever's the matter darling? Has something dreadful happened?'

'No. Not at all. I just want you to know that I will never, ever take you for granted and I'm so happy to share my life with you,' I sob.

Tom, being the practical down-to-earth sort of guy, turns to Allegra and asks for two mugs of coffee. I am so relieved to be back in my own time with my family. It will be such a relief to have all the technology I was so used to before my sojourn into the past.

I know that people say that when you die, key moments from your life flick through your mind. Well, I'm fairly sure that I am not dead but suddenly in my mind's eye I see my flatmates laughing and joking round the dinner table; the horrible homophobic bloke in the pub garden; that classroom of girls laughing at me; the London street markets buzzing with activity; Florence and Sylvia working hard in the office; Pete and Sue's happy wedding day; Jimi Hendrix on stage at the Isle of Wight festival and Andy giving me the tee-shirt. Oh no! No! Andy will be waiting for me at the coffee shop.

I realise with a shock that trying to explain all this to Tom is far too complicated. While I was away, I had no doubt that if I returned to my own time, I would be able to tell him everything that happened but now I am not sure. I feel as if I have been unfaithful, which of course I have.

I also realise that I am worried about leaving that old life behind, without a word to anyone. I try to pull myself together and turn to Tom, smiling as he hands me my coffee.

'So, what have you been up to then?' I ask, hoping for some clarity about my absence.

Tom looks puzzled. 'I've only been gone about twenty minutes, sweetheart. I've taken the boys to Mum and Dad's for a sleep-over, remember?'

Obviously, this isn't giving me any useful answers. I try once more, 'You know when you dropped the plate at breakfast?'

Tom looks puzzled for a moment. 'Oh, yes. Yesterday morning.'

'Well, I cannot remember anything that has happened since then.' This is an outright lie but it's the easiest way to explain my reaction.

'I suppose you have been overdoing it recently,' said Tom. 'Maybe you need a few days off or a visit to the doctors? You really need a break and some time to relax.' I nod as I sip my coffee.

'How about we go out tonight? It's a perfect opportunity while the boys have a sleepover at Mum and Dad's! Shall I book a table at San Lorenzo?'

Frankly, it's the last thing I feel like, given my recent experiences. In the absence of any alternatives I smile my agreement.

'While the weather is good, we could go for a walk in Cannizaro Park this afternoon,' I suggest.

'Hmm I suppose so. Whatever gave you that idea? I don't think we've ever been there. Still, we could check it out so we can take the boys sometime.' I make a quiet mental note to myself that if we do go to the Park not to reveal I have been there before, even if it was in 1970.

My head is still whirling so I excuse myself and head for the shower, explaining that I feel grubby having handled the jumble sale clothing. After all, I haven't had a shower for five months!

Upstairs, I grab my iPhone which is sitting on the dressing table. A quick look at Facebook, Instagram and WhatsApp shows that nothing, absolutely nothing has happened in my twenty-first century world since I last checked.

So, we leave Jane in the shower, washing away the last few months…

❖

I am sitting on the seat outside Wimbledon station, wondering what exactly I am doing here.

'Is there a problem, madam?' said a young policewoman as she walked towards me. I suppose I must have looked a bit disorientated.

'I'm fine thank you. I felt dizzy for a moment, so I thought I should sit down until the faintness passed.'

I stood up and headed purposefully towards the library. I would not want her to think I was "loitering with intent" or soliciting!

Once inside I looked vacantly at the shelves until I spotted a travel book about Canada. That will be ideal to give me some background for my visit to Toronto which is coming up this summer. I decide that this is all I need today, take the book to the librarian on the desk, borrow it and head for home.

Angie is in the kitchen when I open the door. She has just made a pot of tea and she offers me some. We take our mugs into my room for a chat.

'I assume the boiler man did come then?'

'Yes. It took him ages but eventually he figured out it needed a new diaphragm. I've left the docket that I signed on the hall table. Anyway, how did your interview go?'

'Seemed to be alright. They were talking about a vacancy in the Croydon branch, so I think that's what I might be offered. Pete will be pleased!'

'Great. Congratulations! I hope it's a good branch to be posted to for your first management position. Maybe you and Pete will be able to meet up at lunchtimes in future? By the way, I've been thinking, Angie. When Kate moves out, we need to find a new flatmate fairly quickly if we are not going to pay the extra rent ourselves.'

'Yes. I've been thinking about that too. Any suggestions?'

'Well, I did mention the possibility to several colleagues at school. I'm not sure anyone was that interested but you never know.'

'If you chase that up after the Easter holidays that would be good. Any plans for this afternoon?'

'Not really. I've got some lesson planning to do and I need to write to my aunt and uncle in Canada, just to confirm my trip details.'

We leave Jane, sitting at her desk, pen in hand and in the midst of her travel plans…

⁘

'Are you alright, dear?' said the woman with several bags of shopping and two toddlers in tow.

'Thank you. I'm fine now. I just felt a bit faint so I thought it best to sit down until I felt better.'

'Bye then.'

I shook my head, blinked vigorously and checked my watch again. It is only ten past eleven so I'm sure Andy won't be too concerned. I head steadily towards the café.

Andy stood up the minute I got in the door and gave me a massive hug. 'Jane. How good to see you! I know it's only been a few days but I really have missed you.'

'Me too, Andy. How's your Mum?'

'She seems to be on the mend now. She came out of hospital on Wednesday and has been given medication and advice on her diet. Dad is relieved to have her home too.'

We sat companionably drinking coffee and enjoying a slice of Victoria sponge cake together.

'I see you are still wearing the Isle of Wight tee-shirt!'

'Of course. Although I have washed it since we got back, you know!'

'And if I am not rushing things too much, what do you think about us replacing it with something more permanent?'

'I would need to think about that Andy.'

'I would like to meet your parents soon too.'

I smiled my agreement.

'I'm not ready to make big plans yet Andy but we could perhaps think about you taking on Kate's flat?'

'Sounds good to me.'

We leave Jane and Andy making happy plans for their future together…

28. Thoughts from the author

"If you had your life again, what would you do differently?" Our answers may often differ depending on the stage of life that the question is asked.

And yet we are making decisions all the time that will impact on what happens next and what will happen in our future. Turn right? Or turn left? Take the new job opportunity? Stay in the current job? Make the best that one can of this relationship? Or break up and look for better? Sometimes the smallest adjustment to the path one is taking can lead to extraordinary changes. Isn't that wonderful!

Even Fate, ascribed as the development of events outside a person's control which is considered by some people as being predetermined by a supernatural power, is actually affected by whether you decide to act upon your intuition or gut feeling or whether you wait to see what happens if you don't.

As human beings we do have a lot of choices. How, where and to whom we are born are not included, but thereafter the way that one deals with those circumstances is largely within one's purview.

The 1960's and 70's were, for many, a time of hope and a time when self-determination ruled. For those who can remember those days, it seemed that the sun was always shining and young people were free to do whatever took their fancy. The truth is that these were also times of terrible hardship, unrest and sadness. Our memories are not always an honest record of the past. They do, however, offer a very useful marker to assess what great strides have been made by the human race as well as the appalling errors we should never have committed. Let us hope we can learn from all of these as we take every brave step into the future.

If we understand our past, we can understand who we are. And if we can understand who we are we can decide what kind of future we want. There is always a choice to be made, imperfect though it may be, at least we have a choice.

If you enjoyed reading *14 Viney Hill*, I would be delighted if you would consider writing a short review for me. You can do this on https://www.amazon.co.uk. Reviews are very important for authors, as well as for anyone wondering whether to order a book, so any way in which you can help is much appreciated!

I have written three other books, all of which are available via Amazon or to order through any good bookseller. My books are held in the British Library and in some local libraries. They are available in both paperback format and e-book editions. Further information on the books can be found on the following pages.

You can also checkout my Facebook author page www.facebook.com/carolesusansmith which provides news, updates and information about current activities.

If you would like to send me any comments, feedback or criticism you can message me on the Facebook page or send an email to carolesusansmith@pnwriter.org I love to hear from readers!

TravelWorks by Carole Susan Smith

From the age of nineteen Carole decided that travelling to other countries was a lot of fun. She realised that she would need time and money to do more of this. Discovering that the nine-to-five life was definitely not for her, she decided to look for jobs that paid her to travel while working.

Some of her travels have been to places that others might not choose for a holiday or even a short break. Some places, such as Siberia in mid-winter and the Middle East in the height of summer, were encountered in the least propitious seasons.

Her fascinating adventures over the last forty years reflect changes in politics and society as well as in travel itself.

This book of stories, diaries and reflections is for fellow travellers and armchair travellers alike who will appreciate that travel is education and entertainment wrapped up in a colourful package.

HomeWorks by Carole Susan Smith

Carole's first book took the reader to Yekaterinburg, Gaza City, Goteborg and Taipei with various other destinations in between. Whilst Southampton, Manchester, Bristol, Glasgow, Caernarfon, London and Leeds are not as obviously exotic, you may be surprised by some of her adventures nearer to home.

As you accompany Carole on her journeys you will discover why packing a torch on a business trip can get you into trouble and how a jacuzzi makes a good meeting room. Spending time with oil executives speaking six different languages poses no problems for her but trying to understand their technical language does. You may wonder why ninety men were determined to address her as Your Majesty or how come she was standing on a desk quoting Middle English.

Her excuse is she's never been afraid to try something different but you will have to read the whole book to make sense of this!

Oh, and another thing… by Carole Susan Smith

Whether you are applying for a job or in conversation with someone you don't know well, sooner or later you will be asked about your hobbies and interests. Having penned two books about travelling and work life, I thought I should complete the trilogy by confessing to some of the slightly odd things I have done for pleasure.

These include cycling, which didn't end well: "What was intended to be a stylish wheelie manoeuvre across the loose gravel turned into more of a flying circus demonstration".

You will also discover much about outdoor exploits, including caving, climbing and long-distance walking.

In ***Oh, and another thing…*** you will have another opportunity to read a light-hearted book about all the other things I forgot to tell you in ***TravelWorks*** and ***HomeWorks!***